# ROOTS IN THE DUST

# ROOTS IN THE DUST

CAROL ANN MARTIN

This book is a work of fiction based on true events. Names and characteristics of people and places have been changed.

# Contents

# 1

# Chet

Chet tipped his straw hat a little further down his forehead to try to block out some of the sun, not that it was much help, since the glare off of the concrete was worse than the sun beating down on his head. It was August and hot as hell in Grove, and he couldn't wait until he had his business done in town so he could get back out to the ranch. The truck was already loaded with feed, he was just waiting now for the banker to get back from lunch and sign his paperwork. After three seasons of feeding calves and selling them, he had finally paid off his property. So, now, maybe after this season he could keep a little cash for himself.

He was careful with his money. That's how at the ripe old age of (almost) eighteen he was getting the title to his forty acres, free and clear. It hadn't been easy. Getting the bank to loan him the money at fifteen hadn't been the hard part, he had been taking small loans to buy supplies for his yard mowing business since he was twelve and had letters of credit showing that he had always paid them back. No, the hard part had been saving every penny that wasn't needed for the cows to pay on the loan. That meant relying on his mother and his stepfather for everything. Now, it's not unusual for a teenager to live with his parents and rely on them for food, shelter, etc... but his mother? Oh, she made it a challenge. There was just no pleasing the old broad.

He worked hard; he followed the rules (at least as far as she knew) but it was never enough. And the old man was worse. J.T. had always resented raising children that weren't his, though he would never have admitted it in public. He had his standing in the community to think of, and that was all that really mattered to him. Living under their roof had been rough. The next goal he had set for himself was getting some kind of shack on that hunk of property, so he could be out from under that roof.

His sister, Ginny, had felt the pressure, too. That's why she had saved her money from every baby-sitting or housekeeping job she had ever done and bought a Greyhound ticket the minute she turned eighteen. She headed west and didn't stop 'til she saw the ocean. Well, not quite, but close. She was in Bakersfield. He missed her somethin' fierce, but he understood. He got a letter every week or so. She seemed to be doing ok. He just wished she hadn't had to leave him to deal with the parents on his own.

So, just a little while longer until he could get this batch of calves sold. He had paid off his loan, bought calves and feed and with any luck he would have enough money to buy the things he still needed to build his shack. He had been stockpiling lumber for a while from the old house he was tearing down off of his mother's property. Most of it was too far gone but he would probably have enough for a small cabin. Nails, tar paper and roof shingles should be all he had to buy to get dried in.

While he waited for the banker's lunch hour to be over, he wandered down the sidewalk in Grove and peered in the shop windows. The Rexall still had a few stools empty at the lunch counter, but he knew he shouldn't give in to temptation. He had tins of Vienna sausages and some crackers in the truck. He turned away and looked down the street just in time to see a pretty girl step out of an old farm truck. She waved the driver away and yelled that she would meet him back there in an hour. Chet got a look at the driver, a boy about his age. He really hoped it was her brother, because he planned to get to know that pretty girl while he still had some time to kill.

"Hey, good-lookin', whatcha got cookin'!" It wasn't an original line, but Hank Williams was always a crowd pleaser.

Pretty-young-thing shaded her eyes with her hand and looked his way. "Do I know you?"

"No, darlin' not yet." She turned away but not before he saw the hint of a smile.

"Can I help you find something? You look lost." He stepped a couple of steps closer to her, closing the gap a little.

"I'm not lost. I've been to Grove before! (Never on her own, but he didn't need to know that.)

Chet got a better look at the girl, now that he was closer. She was skinny, all arms and legs. She had mousy-brown hair and freckles across her nose. She looked like she spent some time outside, she was tanned and fit. Her cotton print dress blew around her legs in the breeze. Her hair was trying to escape the bobby pins holding it away from her face. She wasn't beautiful, really, but she was just, well, lovely. Lovely was the word that came to mind.

"Well, maybe I could walk with you to wherever it is you're going."

She hesitated for a minute, but they were on the street, in broad daylight. It seemed ok.

"Sure", she said, "I was headed to Ben Franklin's to buy some things. My brother will be back to get me in an hour."

Yes, it was a brother! Not a boyfriend. So far, so good.

"My name is Chet by the way."

"I'm Greta"

"Well, howdy Greta. It's nice to meet you!" It really was. Chet was never short of female attention. Whenever he left the ranch, girls seemed to find him. Just over six feet tall, tanned and muscular, people tended to notice him. And it wasn't just his looks. It was in the way he carried himself. Confidence bordering on cocky, but not aloof. Girls tended to swoon.

But not this one. While polite, she seemed to be indifferent to his charms. She walked beside him like she was used to having him there, no big deal. And to say he was intrigued would be selling it short. He was enthralled. And *that* had never happened before. He liked girls just fine. More than fine. But he was usually the one being pursued. This felt very different.

He struggled to keep the conversation going, "Whatcha lookin' for at the Five and Dime?"

"I'm gonna get some new hair pins and some sewing thread and a pack of needles. Maybe something else, if I have enough money."

He ignored the part about having enough money. It was a pretty common conversation because nobody had enough money. He had been born in September 1929, the last good month of the last good year before Wall Street crashed and it all went to hell. Of course, he didn't know anything different, and neither did Greta, but the folks all talked about a time when money wasn't a common topic for conversation.

"You sew?" He asked surprised. She didn't look at all like the hags that came to his mother's quilting circle.

"'course I do. How else would I get clothes?"

"Did you make that dress?"

"Well, sure I did! Ma helped me cut it out because we only had three flour sacks and really needed four, but we nipped and tucked, and it came out ok."

Chet looked her over appreciatively. "I think I like those nips and tucks."

Greta squinted at him; a hard look she gave her brothers when they were teasing her. "I'm not sure what you mean but I'm pretty sure I don't like it."

"Hold on, hold on, I didn't mean nothin'. Just a real pretty dress, that's all."

By this time, they were in front of the Ben Franklin's. Grove wasn't exactly what you'd call a *big* town.

"You comin' in?"

"Nah, I got business down at the bank."

Greta was a little disappointed, but curious, too. What bankin' business did this fella have? She had never even seen what the bank looked like inside.

Chet saw his opportunity slipping away so he thought fast, "I suppose you heard about the street dance in Starkville tomorrow night?"

"Sure, they have it every year the night before the rodeo starts."

"Well, was you thinkin' of bein' there?" Chet didn't know what he was even thinking. He *hated* going to the events in Starkville. His mother and J.T. would be there for sure.

"Yeah, most likely. My folks like to go and take us kids. We can't all afford tickets to the rodeo, but the street dance and the parade are free. Ma will probably fry a chicken and make some tater salad so we can have our dinner there in the square."

"Well... I was thinkin' I might go this year. Maybe I will see you there."

"Maybe you will."

"Maybe we could dance to one or two songs."

"Maybe we could."

Greta was starting to have fun now. At first this big handsome cowboy came off a bit cocky but now he was patting his foot and looking like one of her brothers when they got caught stealin' biscuits. She grinned at him before she turned to go in the store.

"I guess it's a date then." Chet twirled on his boot heel and walked toward the bank.

Greta grinned and opened the door to the five and dime.

# 2

# Greta

When Greta woke up this morning, at first, she pulled the pillow over her head, dreading another day in the hay field. She was sore and tired and wishing she had never started that job. Then she remembered they finished late last night, and Mr. Johnson had paid them all! It's no wonder she didn't remember. They had been putting hay in the barn by moonlight last night and it was close to midnight when she fell into bed. But remembering that she had money to spend that was all her own, and that Bill was driving her to town today when he went for feed, suddenly her aching muscles didn't ache that much.

At a half cent a bale her week's work had made her just short of $8! Now she would be able to buy a few things all for herself and maybe put away a little for real Christmas presents. Apple picking season was coming up so hopefully she could add to the pot then.

She slipped out of bed wearing her camisole and undies that she had worn under her brother's old coveralls while she was hauling hay. Ma wouldn't be pleased that she didn't change into a nighty, but she had just been so danged tired. She poured cold water from the pitcher into her basin and dunked her flannel washcloth in. She soaped up her face and neck and scrubbed until the skin was pink. She had wiped off before getting in bed, but the dust from that hay was everywhere. She dunked her cloth over and over, scrubbing her whole body until she felt clean and the water in that basin positively was not. She didn't think there was time this morning to do anything about her hair, so she just brushed it and brushed it until she felt like the grit was gone. She tossed the dirty water out of her window onto Ma's rosebushes. Lord knew they would appreciate the drink, dirty or not.

She found a clean slip and pulled it on and then put on her newest flour-sack dress. She had loved this material when she saw it, the flowers reminded her of the fields in springtime. But unfortunately, there had only been three bags with this print. She usually had four to work with. Ma had helped her turn the pattern this way and that until they got it to work. It was a little shorter than her other dresses but as long as Daddy didn't look too hard, it would be ok. She had been making her own clothes and some for her brothers too, for a couple of years, but this year Ma had finally started letting her use the Singer Sewing machine. That machine was the most valuable thing Ma owned, and she was careful with it. Before Greta could use it, she had to teach her how to oil it, how to thread it, how to keep the tension right and how to pump the treadle at a steady pace. That was the hard part. Get going too fast and you might sew through your finger before you could stop it!

Now she looked at herself in the mirror and admired the dress but saw every flaw in herself. She was so scrawny! People called her hair blond, but it wasn't blond like Jean Harlow or Lana Turner. Her hair was more a soft brown color and fine like a baby's. She sometimes tried curling it, but it didn't stay curly. Today she just parted it on the side and stuck some bobby pins in to keep it out of her face.

She slipped her money into her little coin purse and tucked it into the little pocket she and Ma had hidden in the waistband of her dress. Easy to get to but not easy to lose. She smoothed her dress down and took a last look in the mirror and left her room to go help Ma get breakfast on. The sooner she got through the morning chores the sooner she and Bill could leave for town.

As she came out of her room, she saw Ma lighting the burner on the propane cook stove. Lord was she happy every time she saw that match and that blue flame. No need to get up early to get a fire started before breakfast could get cooked. The wood stove was still hooked up in the corner, where it had always been. Honestly, in the winter it was pretty nice to have the old wood burner keeping the kitchen warm and having a pot of coffee warm. But in this heat, it was just wonderful to be able to cook without heating the whole house up. There was talk of getting a propane refrigerator, too, but Daddy didn't see the need since it was just a short walk to the spring, and he had built a nice box in there to keep food cold. The house didn't have electricity yet, it was too far from town, and they hadn't run the wires out here yet. But Daddy probably wouldn't want to pay for that either. He wasn't mean with money; he just didn't see a reason to waste it.

Ma looked up and saw Greta coming out of her room. "Well, ain't you a picture this mornin' Sis? Are you happy to be done in the hay field?"

"Oh, so happy! It's too hot to work like that!"

"Yeah, too bad they don't cut hay in the wintertime huh Sis?"

"Yeah, too bad. You want me to get biscuits started?"

"Nah, I'm thinking it's a bit warm to bake biscuits this morning. Let's eat some potatoes instead." Greta grabbed some potatoes out of the bin and started to peel them. She noticed the bin was getting low. Later she would have to run down to the root cellar and bring some up.

After Greta helped Ma get the breakfast started, she slipped out the screen door and threw some scraps to the chickens. It was blissfully cool on the back porch; it was still in the shade and a little bit of breeze was coming through. She took a minute to enjoy it, knowing it was going to be another scorcher today.

Bill came around the corner brushing the dust off of his Levis before he stepped into the house.

"Are you going to be ready to go when I am?"

"Yeah, I'll be ready. I'm ready now!"

"Must be nice. I still have to get that west fence back up before I can turn the cows out. Has Ma got breakfast ready? I was hoping I could eat before I head out that way."

"It's almost ready. Coffee is done if you want a cup."

"Where are Walter and Gene?"

"Ma said after they got the milkin' done, they went out with Daddy to try to fix that pump for the stock tank. They should be heading in for breakfast."

Ma stepped out on the back porch, "Y'all get in and wash yer hands." She started pulling the rope to clang the big dinner bell. It was loud enough to hear it almost anywhere on the farm. Daddy and the boys would be in soon.

After breakfast, Greta took the buckets and headed out to the pump. She brought both buckets back in and set one of them on the stove to warm up for the dishes. She muddled through cleaning up the kitchen and waited for Bill to get done so they could go to town. While she was excited to have money of her own to spend, she was more excited about getting out to go do something! Even more exciting was that today it was just her and Bill. Daddy was busy and he needed Bill to go get feed for him. He had been reluctant to let Greta go with, but Ma had talked him around.

"She's sixteen years old, Earl. You're gonna have to let her out of your sight someday. You have been letting Bill go to town by himself since he could drive the truck."

"Yeah, but Bill ain't a girl."

"Don't you start that again! A sixteen-year-old girl can walk down the street in Grove and walk into a store just fine! I don't know what you think is gonna happen."

"Yeah, and you don't want to know neither", he muttered under his breath. But in the end, he gave his permission.

So, finally, after waiting all morning and after a hot, dusty drive in the farm truck, Bill was pulling up to the curb in Grove to let Greta out. He had told her it would probably only take him a half hour to load feed, so she had better hurry. Greta was having none of that! So, when she got out of the truck, she made a point of letting him know she would meet him in an *hour.*

She whirled around to walk away and heard someone say, "Hey good lookin' whatcha got cookin?" She turned to see who was speaking and looked right into the bluest eyes she had ever seen. And those eyes were looking right back at her. He was talking to *her!*

"Do I know you?" was all she could get to come out. She almost choked when he said, "No darlin', not yet". But then he said something about her lookin' lost and snapped her out of her shyness. Did he think she was a *kid?*

"I'm not lost! I've been to Grove before." He had moved in closer and was looking her over. She didn't really object because she was looking at him pretty hard, too. Lord, he was handsome! Taller even than Daddy! She struggled to look away and then he asked her if he could walk her to wherever she was going.

"Sure", she said, "I was headed to Ben Franklin's to buy some things. My brother will be back to get me in an hour."

"My name is Chet by the way."

"I'm Greta"

"Whatcha lookin' for at the five and Dime?"

She told him she planned to get some new hair pins and some sewing thread and a pack of needles. It all seemed really dumb, but she didn't know what else to say.

"You sew?"

Didn't everybody? Even her brothers could sew a button or patch their jeans.

"'course I do. How else would I get clothes?"

"Did you make that dress?"

"Well, sure I did! Ma helped me cut it out because we only had three flour sacks and really needed four, but we nipped and tucked, and it came out ok."

Chet looked her over appreciatively. "I think I like those nips and tucks."

Now Greta just felt like she was being teased. There was something about the way he was looking her up and down that she didn't quite understand. "I'm not sure what you mean but I'm pretty sure I don't like it."

"Hold on, hold on, I didn't mean nothin'. Just a real pretty dress, that's all."

She stopped in front of the Ben Franklin's store

"You comin' in?"

"Nah, I got business down at the bank."

Well, that was fun while it lasted. She turned to walk into the store.

"I suppose you heard about the street dance in Starkville tomorrow night?" What was this? He was asking her about the street dance?

"Sure, they have it every year the night before the rodeo starts", she answered slowly, not really knowing where this was going.

"Well, was you thinkin' of bein' there?"

"Yeah, most likely. My folks like to go and take us kids. We can't all afford tickets to the rodeo, but the street dance and the parade are free. Ma will probably fry a chicken and make some tater salad so we can have our dinner there in the square." Why was she babbling? He didn't care if Ma made chicken.

"Well... I was thinkin' I might go this year. Maybe I will see you there."

"Maybe you will."

"Maybe we could dance to one or two songs."

"Maybe we could."

Greta was surprised to see him start looking a little red in the face.

"I guess it's a date then."

Greta stopped short before she opened the door to the store and watched Chet walk away. A date! Whoo-ee Daddy better not hear him say that. Daddy didn't mind so much if she danced a few dances with the boys at the street dance, heck she would probably dance with her brothers and their friends mostly. But date? Daddy would blow sky high if he thought that cowboy was sniffin' around her like *that*! But date? Greta was grinning pretty big when she walked into the five and dime.

# 3

# Street Dance

Chet arrived at the street dance later than he meant to. He had waited for his mother and JT to leave before he started getting cleaned up to go. If he had made them aware he was going, JT would have insisted he ride with them to save on fuel. "I buy my own damned gas anyway ya old fool" he muttered to himself as he walked to the creek. He didn't have time to haul in water for a bath now and honestly a dunk in the creek sounded pretty refreshing after another hot day.

He stripped off and dove in the deep pool and let the water close in over his head for a moment before he found his footing and started using the bar of soap he'd brought with to lather his hair. Making quick work of washing he gathered his clothes and walked back to the house using the inside of his shirt to towel his hair dry. He hoped he was not rubbing more dirt in than he had washed out, but he had forgotten to grab a towel when he went to the creek.

Back at the house, he hurried into his clean "town" clothes and put on his good pair of boots. He crammed his good Stetson on his head and went out the door. One thing he could say for his mother and JT. They might not spend money on many things but what they did buy was good quality. His mother would say there was no value in buying cheap goods. So, he had good clothes and nice boots.

When he got to the dance, the Sorghum Hill Boys were already on their third song and folks were dancing. The streetlights were just flickering on as the sunset was casting long shadows from the buildings surrounding the square. He looked around, saw some people he knew and tipped his hat to a few. It took him a few minutes to lay eyes on the pretty little gal he'd met in Grove the day before. Partially because she was still sitting with her folks and partially because her hair was curled and pulled back in a headband.

Greta saw Chet as soon as he walked onto the street, but she tried not to look too obvious. Instead, she poked Bill in the side and said, "Are we just going to sit here all night?" Walter and Gene were already off at the other side of the square with the other boys their age. They weren't much interested in the dance, but they enjoyed getting to run wild with the other kids for a while.

"Go on if you want to," Bill said as he reached for another piece of pie. Ma slapped his hand and said, "Take your sister over there and dance with your friends, Bill. There will still be pie later."

Greta jumped up and pulled Bill to his feet. She held on to his hand and made a beeline for the side of the street where Chet stood, stopping just short of there to talk to a group of Bill's friends. Tom, Bill's buddy since grade school, asked Greta if she wanted to dance and they jumped in on the waltz that had just started. Greta caught Chet's eye and nodded to him, and he nodded back.

When the song ended Chet just happened to be standing near where Greta and Tom were leaving the dancing area. He held out a hand toward Greta and asked, "May I have this dance, ma'am?"

"Yes sir, you may", she answered brightly, and they fell in at the start of the next song, this one a two-step. It was a lucky stroke on the two-step. Chet could dance a couple of other dances, but the two-step was one he didn't have to think about, so he was more comfortable talking. He was a good leader, and Greta fell into step with him like they had been dancing together for years.

"So, that's your folks over there?"

"Yeah, that's Ma and Daddy. My little brothers are over on the other side of the square screaming with the other kids."

Are y'all going to the Rodeo tomorrow night?

"Nah, I told you, Ma and Daddy won't go to the stuff that costs money. It's too much to buy tickets for the whole family."

"Have you ever been to the rodeo?"

"No"

"Well, I reckon I could pay for a ticket for you if you wanted to go tomorrow night."

"Oh gosh, really? She squealed and then her smile faded. "I doubt Daddy would like that."

"Well, I guess we could ask and find out."

"Oh, I'd better ask by myself. I'm not sure how he will take it if you come over."

When the song ended, Greta stepped back away from Chet. "Do you want me to go ask now?"

"Might as well. I'll go buy us a couple of bottles of Coke."

"Ok. I'll come back as soon as I can."

Greta practically ran back to where Ma and Daddy had been sitting watching the dancers. Daddy was looking at the folks dancing over by the bandstand, but she knew he hadn't taken his eyes off of her for very long. That was the curse of being the only girl. Daddy protected her from everything. Other girls her age could wear lipstick, but not Greta. Other girls had been out on dates with boys to picture shows, but Greta couldn't go anywhere unless Ma or Daddy were going to be there.

Hey Sister, you having fun? You're not all danced out already, are you?" Ma teased as Greta sat on the blanket beside her.

"No, but I have a question for Daddy."

"What's that Sister?"

Daddy was waiting for her to speak up, but she couldn't read his expression. Folks always said that Earl Reddington was wasted being a farmer, he could have made a fortune as a riverboat gambler with his poker face. But the only cards Earl ever touched was the deck he played Ol' Sol with.

"Well, Daddy', she hesitated while she gathered her nerve, "We weren't going to the rodeo tomorrow night, were we?

"Sister, you know I'm not spending money to watch men ride horses. We can watch that at home."

"Yeah, that's what I thought, but what I was really wondering is, if I had a ticket bought for me, could I go?"

"And just who would be paying for this ticket?" Daddy asked, sitting up a little straighter and leaning toward Greta.

She didn't have trouble reading him now. He was *not* happy.

From where he stood with his friends, Bill had been watching since Greta had made a beeline for their parents. When he saw Daddy puffing up, he told his buddies, "Be right back" and headed toward the picnic spot. Greta was a spoiled pain in his.... side, but he also knew that Daddy kept her too close to home. The little idiot was never gonna grow up if daddy had his way. He thought he would see if he could help, if only to keep the ride home from being too awful.

As he approached, he heard Greta say, "Well Daddy, Chet has offered to buy a ticket for me because I've never been to the rodeo and..."

Before she could finish, Daddy was saying, "who is this Chet? That saddle-tramp you were dancing with? Is he just in town for the rodeo? Because I won't have you..."

"Daddy, he's not a saddle-tramp, "Bill cut in. Seems like he got there right in time. Daddy was about to tell us all again about how you can't trust a saddle-tramp. He had strong opinions on the subject since he had worked on the big ranches in Oklahoma and Texas as a youth. Apparently, he was the only trustworthy saddle-tramp that had ever existed.

Daddy broke off and looked at Bill, so he continued, "That's Chet Masters. He's local. His Ma teaches at the Starkville school."

"I don't know no teacher named Masters"

"That's his name. His Ma is Mrs. Smith."

Ma broke in then; I didn't know Mrs. Smith had a son. I thought the Smith's didn't have children."

"Well, *they* don't I reckon. Mrs. Smith had kids before she married Mr. Smith. I think they were half grown before they moved here."

"How do you come by this information?" Daddy wanted to know.

"I keep my ears open when I'm at the feed store. Those old men gossip like old women."

Daddy thought it over. "His Ma being a schoolteacher don't mean he's not a saddle-tramp. And how come them boys to be gossiping about Mrs. Smith anyway? What's to gossip about?"

"That's the thing Daddy. That's what I'm trying to say. They ain't been talking about *her*. Well, I mean they have but mostly just talking about Chet. He ain't a saddle-tramp, Daddy. He's a *cattleman* with his own place."

"His own place? That boy can't be more 'n twenty ortwenty-one. How'd he get his own place."

"I heard he's eighteen. And he got his own place by buying it himself. I heard them say yesterday, while I was loading feed, that he was over at the bank getting his loan paid off and his title in his name. He had a truck load of feed sitting there. He buys and sells calves every year. They said he's been getting top dollar because his calves get grain with their hay and pasture. Folks and have been fighting over buying his steers because the beef is so good. So, he ain't a saddle-tramp Daddy. He's a rancher and a good one, too."

Earl sat back and digested what Bill had just told him. That was pretty impressive if it was true. But it still didn't mean he wanted Greta anywhere near him. Maybe he was just eighteen, but Greta was just sixteen. A baby.

The baby in question was digesting some information, too. So that's why he was going to the bank yesterday! She had almost blurted that out but caught herself. Daddy would have wanted to know where she got her information, too.

"So, why are we talking about Chet anyway?", Bill asked. He hadn't quite got there for that part of the conversation.

Ma jumped in before Daddy could. "Chet has kindly offered to buy Greta a ticket for the rodeo tomorrow night. Now, Daddy is considering if it's a good idea."

Bill knew that Daddy wasn't going to think it was a good idea. He also knew that he didn't really like telling Greta no. So, Bill offered, "I was thinking of going to the Rodeo tomorrow night myself. I have money from hay hauling. I could take Greta if Chet paid for the ticket. Then we can all sit together."

Ma gave Bill a little wink as a thank you. "Now Earl, that seems like a fair idea to me."

Earl thought it over for a minute and could see that he really had no easy way to say no. "If Bill is going to be there to keep an eye on you, I reckon there is no reason you can't go."

"Thank you, Daddy!" Greta jumped up and looked over to where Chet was standing, trying to pretend he hadn't been watching her the whole time.

"Well, go on. Go tell him", Ma said and shooed the youngsters away.

Earl said, "I don't know why a man that works for his money would want to spend it on buying tickets for someone else."

Ma said quietly, "Oh, I think you do..."

# 4

# Rodeo

As Chet finished up the evening chores and started getting ready to head off for the Rodeo, he was thinking about how the dance had gone last night. Thankfully, by the time he had gotten there his mother and JT had been fully involved in discussion with the group of people from their church that they had picnicked with. They had brought folding tables and chairs and had sat a little apart from the crowd like the uppity snobs they were.

Chet had never figured out where the snobby attitude came from, they had it better than some folks, but they weren't rich. But as Mother would point out, they were *educated*. Well, except for him, the big disappointment. He could figure how much calves would cost, how much to feed them, how much profit he was likely to see and plan the whole year out. But if you asked him to show on paper how he got there, he got frustrated.

But last night, they had seen him there and nodded and then ignored him the rest of the night. Thank God, at least no one waved him over to ask why they hadn't been seeing him in church lately or any other such awkward thing. Maybe they had all given up on him. Good.

He smiled when he remembered Greta bouncing back over to tell him that she could go to the rodeo. She didn't really have to tell him; he could see as soon as she started over that she was grinning from ear to ear. She brought her brother Bill, to introduce him. He had seen Bill around and knew of him, but he had never really talked to him.

He and Bill were the same age, Bill had just graduated high school last spring. Folks always kind of wondered why he didn't go to school in Starkville, and he usually just let them wonder. He had fought his way through 9$^{th}$ grade and when they moved here, he just didn't start tenth grade. Not that it had been that easy. JT had knocked him around pretty good saying that he was an embarrassment to the family. Chet pointing out that he and JT weren't family had not been wise. But he did all the farm chores that JT could throw at him as well as keeping up with his calves over on his place. Since he was basically an unpaid farmhand and didn't go into town often enough for anyone to know his business, JT soon calmed down. It helped that looked older, so not that many people came right out and asked if he should be in school.

That first year with the place and the calves had been rough. JT was determined to not make it easy on him, so he piled the work on. The property that he bought was joined to his mother's and JT's place on one side so fixing that fence to keep his calves in could be considered one of his chores. But working on the other three sides had to be done on his "free" time. Unfortunately, a lot of that free time was spent rounding up calves that had gone through the fence he hadn't repaired yet. But as they got accustomed to being fed every day, they quit wandering as much and eventually it all worked out. But the costs of that first year barely left him enough to pay his annual loan payment and enough to roll back into calves for the next year. But year two left him some wiggle room. It was all luck, you never knew when a whole herd might get sick, or wolves would take down a calf or two and then you could lose it all. But that was the gamble. That was also why even on a good year, that money had to be held back in case of an emergency.

But he didn't think the cost of a rodeo ticket or two was going to cut into his funds too much, and at least the farm loan was paid for good.

He and Bill and Greta had agreed to meet at the main entrance of the rodeo grounds about an hour before the Grand Entry was set to start, Since Bill was driving Greta, Chet had an idea. He had saddled Smoke, his big black gelding and was going to ride to the arena instead of driving the truck. It was only about three miles. JT would be thrilled he wasn't wasting any gasoline.

He wore basically the same clothes as last night, switching out his shirt for the one with pearl snaps. His Levis were tucked into his tall boots and of course, he wore his Stetson.

He set out for the town as his mother was walking home. School was set to start next week, and she had been in, preparing her classroom. One of the other teachers dropped her off at the blacktop, but most folks didn't bring their cars down this dirt road. His mother didn't drive so during the school year, she rode the school bus, which stopped at the blacktop, leaving her to walk the mile in and out. In the worst weather, JT would drive her to the bus stop. He was a sweetheart that way.

"Where you off to? You and Smoke both look mighty fine!"

"Oh, I thought I would head up and see if that rodeo is any good. Maybe let Smoke visit with the out-of-town horses."

"Well, I think you and Smoke both deserve to do a little visiting. Have a good time, but don't keep Smoke out too late, he has work tomorrow."

He nodded and rode on. Hell yeah, Smoke had work tomorrow. The only time he had off was when Chet was using the truck. Usually if Chet was working Smoke was, too.

By the time he made it to the rodeo grounds, it was just about time to meet Bill and Greta. Chet went to the entry gate and paid for two tickets, which were handed right up to him. These people knew cow-boys don't dismount without good reason. The ticket seller asked him, "Are you riding in the Grand Entry? All are welcome."

"Well, I hadn't thought of it, but I might."

"If you decide you want to just get in line when the music starts. All you have to do is follow the horse in front of you, the color-guard sets the pattern."

"Sounds good. Thanks."

It was about then that he saw Greta and Bill pulling in. They got waved over to the visitor parking and were looking for a spot to park. Chet headed Smoke over to the lot, hoping they hadn't seen him yet. He kind of wanted to see Greta's reaction to him on Smoke.

He came up behind their truck just as Greta was getting out. At first, she didn't see him, just that there was a horse standing very close to the truck. Then she looked up. Her eyes widened and then she grinned that grin where every one of her perfect teeth showed.

"Hey Chet! Who is this handsome creature?" She walked right up and gave Smoke a good rub, right under the bridle.

"This is Smoke. And he seems mighty happy to meet you." By that point Smoke was moving his head so Greta could scratch the other side of his face, it felt soooo good.

Greta laughed, "He does seem fairly pleased," she said as Smoke proceeded to bury his head in her middle.

Chet laughed, too. "Yeah, poor old guy, never gets any attention."

Bill was leaned against the truck watching this interaction. "Nice horse."

"Thanks, I like him. I was actually wondering if Greta would like to ride with me in the Grand Entry?"

Bill said, "If there are two things Greta likes, it's horses and showing off, so I'd say it's a good bet".

Greta turned beet red. "Hush, nobody asked you" she said, giving her brother that look that Chet already knew meant she was ready for a fight.

But when she turned to him, she was all sweet and innocence and a little disappointed looking. "I didn't exactly wear riding pants."

"That's ok, you can ride up here in front of me, sort of side-saddle." He had taken his work saddle off of Smoke and tacked him up with his showy parade saddle. It was very roomy, so if he slid back there was space and it had a low horn, not like his roping saddle.

"I don't know" Greta started to say about the time that Bill gave a nod to Chet and just handed Greta up to him. Before she could really object, she was settled in, in front of Chet, with her dress draped over her legs. Chet said if you just kind of hook your right leg over the front of the saddle you can face forward a little more. She rearranged a little and pulled her skirt to cover as much leg as she could. Fortunately, she had worn a pleated skirt so she was able to arrange it so it looked nice.

Greta had been riding since she was two, so she was comfortable enough on horseback, but sitting sideways in front of Chet was different. First of all, she was propped on the saddle and not in control at all. Second, and this was the big one, she was leaned against Chet with his arms wrapped around her. A boy she just met two days ago. But, other than her being a little nervous, it just felt so right.

Chet took her for a big loop around the arena and parking area. It wasn't time to line up for the Grand Entry yet. As they rode, she saw a few girls from school and gave them a little wave. She could see them look at her in shock and then start talking to each other behind their hands.

Greta smiled a little to herself. Let 'em gossip. She was always the odd one out in school. Her clothes were all homemade, she wasn't allowed to date or wear lipstick, and she felt like she was just missing out on things. They weren't mean exactly, but they talked over her head like she couldn't possibly understand. This would have their tongues wagging!

Chet saw Greta wave at the girls, and he smiled a little, too. His sister Ginny had her share of stories about the girls from their old school. He knew how they could peck a girl to death like a bunch of hens after the runty chick. If this little ride helped Greta out, then he was glad he rode Smoke tonight.

After a couple of rounds of the parking lot, they heard the speakers in the announcer's booth start to crackle and some recorded music started to play. Chet reigned Smoke toward the front gates to take their place in line.

"You still want to do this? You comfortable enough?"

Oh, my leg will be asleep the rest of the evening, but I think it's worth it!"

Chet chuckled. "Well, if you're sure."

Chet nudged Smoke in behind a Palomino Quarter horse and waited to hear the music that would signal the start of the Grand Entry. As "Under the Double Eagle" poured out of the speakers, Chet told Greta to hang on and Smoke stepped out in a pretty trot right on the Palomino's tail. The riders paraded in a pattern in the arena moving pretty quickly to give the audience a good show. Fortunately, Smoke's trot was fairly smooth, and Greta's ride was not as bumpy as it would have been on old Bonnie, the plow horse that they had all learned to ride on.

Greta could see that the girls from school were watching her and were green with envy. She gave another little wave their direction. Chet was probably the most handsome cowboy they had ever seen, and it was Greta riding with him, not them!

Later, with Smoke tied under the bleachers, Chet and Greta climbed up to sit by Bill, just like they had promised Pa. Chet and Bill talked about ranching and horses and seemed to get along really well. Greta could tell that Bill was a little in awe of Chet and she liked that just fine.

Bill invited Chet to come out to their place on Tuesday to look at some calves from their dairy herd. They weren't the beef cattle he usually bought, but they were cheap and would probably do ok if he fed them up. Greta was grateful to Bill for thinking this one up. Daddy would be a lot friendlier to Chet if Bill brought him over *and* he was there to buy calves than he would be if he just came to see Greta.

After the rodeo, Chet led Smoke while he walked Greta over to the truck. Bill busied himself checking under the hood so that they could have a minute alone.

Greta said, "Well, I guess we will be seeing you on Tuesday."

"Yup, seems like."

Greta got shy again and looked down at her feet, "I'll be looking forward to that", she mumbled.

Chet reached out to take her hand and she looked up at him, "I will be, too."

Then he opened the truck door, and she got in as Bill slammed the hood and crawled in the driver's seat.

Bill noticed that Greta didn't talk much on the way home, but she was staring at her hand like she had never seen it before. He just let her be.

# 5

# Ginny

Ginny had learned lesson number one early on, and that was that women don't have many choices in life, so you better make darned sure that you do the best with the ones you get. Her mother hadn't had any choice when she was left a widow with two children at the start of the Depression. When she had married, there had been money to live in town, to buy clothes in a store, and when babies came, they had everything they needed. Not that they were well-off, but they were *town*. As opposed to *country* like both sets of Ginny and Chet's grandparents. Little Ginny had pretty dresses and little Mary Jane shoes and baby Chet was pushed around town in a wicker pram, with a hood to keep the sun out.

But then Papa was just gone one day, his car hit by a truck full of melons. The car was gone, Papa was gone and pretty soon most of the pretty things were gone. Mother had tried to hang on in town, but the house was rented and she soon found out that Papa had been a good provider but not much of a planner. When the crash happened in '29, he, like a lot of folks, thought things would bounce back, so he dipped into the savings he still had to keep up rent and spending like always. But apparently, paying the life insurance or the insurance on the car were unnecessary so he had stopped. By the time he died in the spring of '32, Mother found out there was nothing left. There was no choice for her but to sell what she could and pack up her two children and move back out to the farm with her parents. Since Grandfather and Grandmother Adler still had children at home, Mother being their eldest, they were none too happy to see Mother move back, bringing extra mouths to feed. But they made room, and everybody learned how to do chores to earn their keep.

Mother didn't want that life for herself or the children. When she had left the farm to go get a teaching certificate she had never planned to come back. Then she met Papa and was swept off her feet, so she never finished her schooling. So, that was the second thing little Ginny learned about choices, getting swept off your feet is a foolish one. She learned that when she realized that Mother was going to leave her and Chet with the grandparents while she went back to town and school and her teaching certificate. Ginny begged to go, but Mother said she couldn't take care of children and go to school, which was no doubt true, but that didn't matter to a girl who had just turned six and a boy that was not yet three. So, Mother had felt she had no choice. Well, the way Ginny saw it, she could have stayed in school in the first place.

So, Mother went to live in town while Ginny and Chet stayed on the farm and did chores. Ginny started first grade and was bored to tears by "learning" to read and write. She had been reading since she was three. (Her mother was *almost* a teacher you know) Ginny's "city ways" were different to the children from the local farms. She tried to fit in but just didn't. She had expected to go to the big brick school in town with children her age and instead she was in a one-room school with grades one through eight.

After the first school year, Mother had come back to the farm to work over the summer break. Midway through the summer an argument broke out between Mother and the grandparents that ended with Ginny and Chet, once again, loaded up with everything they owned and moved. This time they went to Papa's parents, Grandma and Grandpa Masters. They said they were delighted to have them, that they should have come there in the first place. From where Ginny was sitting, it was more of the same. Another old farmhouse, miles away from anywhere, chores to be done, a one room schoolhouse in the fall. But Mother hadn't had a lot of choice. There was one difference. All Grandma and Grandpa's children were grown so there weren't Aunts and Uncles to play with or help with the chores. But Grandma and Grandpa didn't have as many to feed either, so they didn't try to farm as much. Just what was needed to survive.

When school started again, Ginny tried again to talk Mother into taking her with her. But it was a half-hearted attempt. She knew she wasn't going anywhere. She was starting to expect that since Papa died, no one had really loved her or Chet, they were just a burden to be passed around. She remembered being pampered and petted and now, no one was cruel, but no one had time for her above what was necessary to keep her fed and clothed. She knew Chet could barely remember Papa, he didn't have much idea of the *before*, but Ginny made sure that if nothing else, Chet would know *she* loved him. It was the two of them for life.

After Mother finished school and finally got that teaching certificate, Ginny was sure that it meant they were going back to town. But that was not to be.

"Why, Mother? Why?!"

"Well Ginny, that's just not how things work. I have applied to be a teacher at some very nice school districts, and I'm sure to get something, but it takes time to get things. For you children to come with me, we would need a house and furniture. I'll be living in a furnished room for a while. And what about Chet?"

"What about him?"

"Well, you would be in school when I was teaching, that would be fine, but Chet doesn't start school till next year. Who will watch him?"

Ginny almost begged to come by herself but realized that would leave Chet all alone. No, she wouldn't do that.

So, another year on the farm with Grandma and Grandpa Masters. Chet was growing into a sturdy young lad. Out of baby clothes and into tiny overalls just like the farmers. He was learning about cows and sheep from Grandpa Masters. And that wasn't all. Chet had learned to cuss pretty well before he started school. As he would say in later years, "if ol' Grandpa Fred was a talkin' he was a cussin'".

The following spring, just after school was out, Mother came home with an announcement: she had married JT Smith, and they were all moving to town! And a big town, too. JT owned a grocery store and they would live in the rooms above it. Ginny would go to a big school and Chet could start first grade in a proper public school.

Ginny had been gob-smacked! Married? Without a word to her children. Not a hint in the letters that she wrote each week, telling them that she loved them and to be good for Grandma and Grandpa. It meant they were finally going back to town. That part was true. But Ginny had imagined it would always be the three of them. She had never imagined Mother being married to anyone but Papa!

Grandma Masters was surprised as well. She thought to see her daughter-in-law married again someday, but she hadn't heard a word of it. To cover her shock, she said, "Well at least you don't need to teach, and you can spend time with your children".

"Oh, JT thinks I should continue teaching. We can use the extra income, and you know I love it. But the children will be in the same school where I teach so we can all be together."

Grandma never shared her opinion, one way or another. It wasn't up to her. Not her choice.

Soon, they were packed up and moving to another new life. They never met JT until they walked into his store in town, after being thoroughly slicked and wiped down by Mother outside. She brought her two precious angels in to meet their new "Papa" with the truck outside waiting to be unloaded with everything they owned.

"JT! I'm home! And here are the children, Ginny and Chet."

Mother squeezed their hands and they both said "Hello Papa" just like mother had them rehearse. That Ginny said it through clenched teeth was barely noticed, because of how fast JT said, "Now, there is no call for that. You will call me JT, like everybody else."

Ginny had no problem with it, that man was *not* her Papa. But she could tell that mother was not as thrilled.

"JT, we talked about this…"

"You talked, I listened and then I decided. Papa will be what my own children call me."

"But JT…"

"Enough, take the children upstairs. I have men coming to unload the truck."

That pretty much set the tone for the next few years, at least with JT. As long as they stayed out of his way, he pretty much forgot they existed. It wasn't much different to what they were used to.

Finally getting to start school in a *real school* in town wasn't everything Ginny had hoped for. While she was too *town* for the country kids, here she was too *country* for the town kids. The work she had done in the country school wasn't up to par with the current curriculum, so she had some catching up to do. But she was smart and caught on fast. For Chet, who had been a country kid as long as he could remember, it was awful. He hated dressing in anything but his overalls, and that wasn't allowed for school wear. His cussing got his mouth washed out more than once before he finally learned to hold his tongue. He struggled to read, and his grades were poor. Ginny felt so bad for him and helped him all she could, but the only time he was ever happy was when they got to go spend summers on the farm with one set of grandparents or the other. Oh, and that happened every year, because when school wasn't in session JT needed Mother's help in the store and saw no need to have children underfoot.

One year slipped into another, following this pattern until the year Ginny graduated high school. She was nearing her eighteenth birthday and was trying to decide what to do next. Should she stay here with mother and JT and go to college or try her chances somewhere else? Well, once again she learned, women don't get many choices. JT made that clear to both her and mother.

JT "surprised" them all at dinner just after Ginny's graduation. "Well, everyone, I have news. I've sold the store!"

"You what?!" Mother nearly stood up from the table before she remembered Ginny and Chet were watching.

She sat back down and calmed herself. "I'm sorry, I must have misunderstood. Did you say you sold the store?"

JT smirked. "It sounds like you understood. I sold the store. Everything. Merchandise, fixtures, building and all.

Mother gasped. "Why, JT, why?" She managed to keep her voice soft, but only just. Chet and Ginny could see she was furious. They had never seen her this furious.

"I've had my eye on a little patch of land in Starkville, AR. Well, I say little, but it's three hundred acres, so a fair piece of land. With the proceeds from the store and the money in the bank I had enough to buy it outright."

"JT, at least half of that money was mine. My salary. My work."

"I spend *our* money as I see fit. I saw fit to quit working in a store every day, taking ration tickets scraping by, when we could own a farm of our own. So, I made this decision.

Ginny looked at her mother and saw how it was. She worked, she made money, she saved and yet she had no choice in how her life would go. Ginny made her decision right then. The only choice she had was to get out now. But she had to talk to Chet first and she had to make a plan. Fortunately, she had never taken JT up on his offer to "store" her money for her in his bank account. She had kept it all hidden, almost every nickel she had ever earned in town or on the farm. Babysitting, cleaning houses, hauling hay, picking berries...all of it saved back for someday. Well, it looked like someday was getting close.

Later that night she met Chet out on the roof over the loading dock at the back of the store. Once they went to bed at night, JT would hear if they took a step out of their bedrooms and was always there to ask why they were up. But in all these years he had never figured out that their windows both opened to this rooftop. It was like having a private balcony. Sometimes they had watched concerts and plays in the park from their perch on the roof. On hot nights they slept out there, being careful to creep back in before dawn.

Chet put his bare foot out the window and crept over to sit by Ginny. "Well, that was a surprise you gotta give him that."

"I thought Mother was going to have a fit. A real one. She looked like her heart might explode."

"You didn't look much better. You aren't going, are you?"

Ginny shook her head. Here she thought she was going to have to break it to him. She should have known that Chet would see everything she saw and come to the same conclusions. Chet didn't get good grades, and a lot of people thought he was slow, but he saw things and he thought fast.

'I'm going alright, but not to Shitville, Arkansas. And you don't have to go either Chet. I've saved all my money, and I know you have saved some. We can go out west and get jobs"

"Aw Ginny, you know I can't. They may not want me around much but there's no way they are just going to let me leave before I'm eighteen. JT wouldn't like the way it looked. Besides that, it won't be as bad for me. I like farmin'. If I can just work on the farm and be left alone, I'll be fine."

Ginny knew it was true. She had her sights set on California. Not LA probably, but somewhere to the north of there maybe. She was ok with never seeing a farm again. She had taken typing classes in high school. She bet she could get a job as a secretary or even go to a secretarial school. But Chet would hate that. She wanted to live in an apartment and hang out with the girls from work and go to the beach on the weekends. There wasn't any part of that for Chet. She could see that. But being away from him was going to be hard. She had been watching out for her baby brother since he took his first steps. But if she was going to make any choices for herself, she had to start here.

Chet watched Ginny as she worked it all out in her head. He had already been thinking on it. He knew how hard it would be for Ginny to leave him, but he couldn't go, even if Mother would let it happen.

"It'll be alright Ginny, really it will. You can write me letters telling me how great things are for you, and I can.... I dunno, draw you a picture of a cow or something." He grinned at her and gave her a little wink.

She rammed her shoulder into his "Hey dummy, you can't pull that with me. I know you can write well enough to write a letter. Save the stupid act for your teachers."

"Well, it ain't all an act. It does take me a powerful long time to write anything, so don't expect much."

"It's not like I'll never be back. I just have to go see what's out there."

"I think once you see what's out there, you ain't comin' back. But really Ginny, it's ok. I knew it would happen. I've always known. You can't stay here. You aren't made for it."

"Gosh Chet. That's the most I've heard you say at once in......ever."

Now Chet shoved her with *his* shoulder. They both fell silent and just looked out over the park, enjoying the time they had left together.

# 6

Making Her Move

Ginny counted her money and made her plans quietly. As Mother and JT packed up to move to Arkansas, Ginny packed, too. She gave away things that she wouldn't need to girlfriends from school. She packed boxes to go to the farm and put them with the other boxes to be loaded on the truck. But in secret, she had purchased two sturdy suitcases and an overnight bag, and in those she put the things she would want with her in California. Mostly clothes, but a couple of books she couldn't live without, her rag doll and a little bit of jewelry. Nothing valuable, just ornaments. In each piece of luggage, she hid some of her savings. Hopefully if she lost luggage, she wouldn't lose it all. She had visited the Greyhound bus station to find out how much her ticket would be and how much luggage she could take. Her two bigger pieces could be stowed in the cargo hold and her bag could stay on her lap, but there was a weight limit on the bigger bags. She waited until Mother and JT were away on errands and got Chet to help her weigh her bags on the scale in the store. To her relief they were both fine. Now to wait.

JT had planned for the takeover of the store by the new owners to be June first. Ginny's eighteenth birthday was May thirtieth. Since most of their things were packed to move, Ginny's birthday dinner was to be at a diner near the store and that suited Ginny just fine. She was going to tell Mother and JT her plans at dinner, and they were less likely to make a fuss in public.

When they were seated and orders had been taken, Chet gave Ginny a little nod of encouragement. She took a deep breath and just blurted, "I'm not going with you to Arkansas!"

Mother said, "What do you mean? How will you get there?"

"I mean, I'm not going at all. I'm going to California."

"Ginny! You can't just decide to go to California! How would you get there? Who would you stay with?"

Then JT chimed in, "Who do you think is paying your way, Missy?"

Count on JT to focus on the important stuff.

"I'm going by Greyhound; I'm staying in an all-girls boarding house at first. And, JT, I'm paying my *own* way. I'm leaving tomorrow, my ticket is paid for."

Mother and JT both sat back in their chairs for a minute, taking in all that they had just heard. Chet watched JT. He could see the wheels turning. He could see JT thinking of how much less it would cost him if he wasn't expected to provide for Ginny, so to his mind, this was all good.

Ginny was watching their mother. It wasn't as easy for her. She could see all the disappointment that she felt, about the move, about JT making her decisions for her but she could also see the guilt. The years that she hadn't made time for her children. And now Ginny was leaving.

"Ginny, I counted on you to help me on the farm. I thought we would spend time together making curtains and making a home there."

"I know Mother, but this is my choice."

"How will we ever get you packed to go in time?"

"It's all done, Mother. I'm packed and have my ticket and I'm ready."

JT chimed in again, "Well it looks like that's settled."

Once JT said it was settled, Mother knew that she had no more say. JT was happy with the way things were, so there would be no help from him.

"Yes, I guess it's settled then, "Mother mumbled quietly, and looked down at the table.

In that moment, Ginny almost waivered. Almost. She did feel sorry that her mother felt so bad, but not sorry enough to give up on the life she wanted for herself. She gave her mother's hand a gentle squeeze and then the waitress arrived with their meal and talk around the table turned to more normal subjects.

In four days, Ginny stepped off of the bus in Bakersfield, CA. She felt dirty, her clothes looked like they had been slept in for days, because well, they *had been,* she was tired and .... she had never felt more alive! She looked at the map drawn on the back of the letter she had received from the owner of the boarding house where she had reserved a room. She had her mail delivered to general delivery, so JT wouldn't poke around in her business, and she had checked with the post office every day, praying the letter would arrive in time. It arrived on her birthday, just in time to let Mother know her plans were set.

The map indicated that the boarding house was a short walk from the bus station, so she set off in that direction. She didn't relish carrying her two bags, overnight bag and pocketbook by herself, but paying cab fare was something she just couldn't afford. So, by wrapping the handle of her purse around the handle of one suitcase and putting the overnight bag under her arm, she was just able to lift both bags. She could do this.

"Excuse me, Miss?" A young man in military uniform was standing near her. "Have you far to go?"

"Oh, no, not far. Just a few blocks."

"Could I help with your bags? I'm going the same way."

"I wouldn't want to be a bother."

"Oh no bother, I just finished with basic training. We've been walking with packs everywhere. This will just help keep me in shape. You'd be doing me a favor!"

Ginny chuckled, "If it's for our men in uniform, how could I refuse?"

He grabbed both large cases and Ginny had to admit, he didn't seem to struggle with the weight nearly as much as she had been.

"I should introduce myself, I'm Danny Armbruster."

"Hello, Mr. Armbruster, I'm Ginny Masters."

"Oh, please call me Danny."

"Ok, Danny, you may call me Ginny. Armbruster, that's a German name, isn't it?"

"Ha. Not everyone knows that. But, yes, it was originally. My people have been here for a long time. Don't worry."

"Oh no, I didn't mean it like that. I'm just interested in names."

"Where is Masters from?"

"Old English. And surprisingly, not because my family *were* masters, but more likely *served* masters. So, I'm likely descended from servants. Seems right."

"That's interesting."

"Oh, Danny, I think you are playing fast and loose with the word interesting. I'm just babbling."

"No, really, it seems like you know what you are talking about."

"Well, thank you for that. And thank you for carrying my bags. I think this is my address." She glanced around and saw a small sign on the doors, confirming that this was her boarding house.

"You're new in town, I guess. Do you know anyone here?"

"Not really."

Danny took a pencil and scrap of paper from his pocket and started scribbling something. "Look, I'm in town for a few days to see my mom before I ship out. If you need anything, this is her address. Seraphina Armbruster. She would help you out if you needed anything."

"Oh my, that is very kind of you."

"Not at all, it's just the way my mother raised me. If I *didn't* offer assistance to a girl alone in town, my mom would have my head!"

Ginny laughed, "It sounds like your mother raised you well."

"She tried. My father died when I was young, so it was hard on her, but she was always there for me."

"She sounds wonderful. My papa died when I was young, also. It can be rough."

"Ginny, I'd like to see you again before I leave. Just to make sure you are settling in ok. Mom's house isn't far from here, so I could drop by tomorrow afternoon. Would that be ok?"

"Well, tomorrow afternoon, I have an appointment with the Dean of Women at Bakersfield College at two."

"That's perfect. How about I come here at one-thirty and I'll walk with you? I grew up here, I know all the shortcuts."

"That sounds wonderful, Danny."

As he walked away, she knocked on the door of what would be her home for the foreseeable future. She was greeted by the landlady and settled into a very agreeable corner room, just up one flight of stairs. So far things were going well.

# 7

# Bakersfield

When Ginny wrote Chet her first letter from Bakersfield, she had a lot to tell him. In the few days she had been there, she had settled into her room, met a few of the girls who lived there and been enrolled for classes in the secretarial department at Bakersfield College. She was going to continue living at her boarding house because with meals included it was her cheapest option. Most of the girls living there also went to college, so it was like their own sorority.

She had seen Danny every day since she got there. He had shown her all over town and even taken her to dinner at his mother's house. While at dinner, his mother told Ginny that she was going to be so lonely with Danny overseas. Ginny had promised to drop in for visits as often as she could. His mother was so sweet and so obviously devoted to Danny that it made her wonder what it would have been like if Papa had never died. Would her own mother have been as devoted if she hadn't had to make a living? She would never know for sure.

She wrote to Chet that her new friend Danny was shipping out tomorrow. She had promised to write to him. He had been so good to her in the short time she had been there. They had gone to one of those photo booths and had their picture taken together. She cut the strip in half and gave Danny two pictures and kept two for herself.

Her classes didn't start until September, so she was starting a job as a waitress to make as much money as she could before then. If she didn't want to work full-time and take classes, she would have to pack some money away. Between meals provided at the boarding house and the shift meal she got at the diner; she didn't have to worry about being fed.

Chet read it all and he was so happy for her. It wasn't that bad here on the farm. At least he didn't feel trapped in town anymore and could wear his jeans or overalls if he pleased. Gosh, he missed Ginny, but it seemed like she was getting everything she wanted.

~ ~ ~

By Ginny's twentieth birthday, she had settled into Bakersfield and couldn't imagine being anywhere else. Her "temporary" room at the girls boarding house had turned out to be a longer stay than anticipated, but she loved the other girls, and the deal was really good.

Ginny had only ever had one or two friends in high school. She was never in town in the summers when the gang was doing things together and she was always a little on the outside. Here, all the girls were from somewhere else and so no one was the odd one out. She felt like she had a house full of sisters.

But Ginny felt like the time had come to move on. She had been looking for a small apartment. She had considered asking one of the girls to be a roommate, but she felt like she was ready for a home of her own.

She had graduated from Bakersfield College's secretarial school and had gotten the first job she applied for. Her typing and shorthand skills were the best in her class. She was starting next week as a personal secretary to an attorney at a big local firm. She would say she felt all grown up, but that didn't seem like a very grown-up thing to say.

She wrote Chet and her mother a letter almost every week. She also wrote to Danny on a regular basis. She could usually write Chet and mother letters during her typing class. Danny's letters she usually wrote sitting at her little desk in her room. She put a lot of thought into those letters. Danny wrote to her as often as he was able, and sometimes he got her letters three or four at once, when they caught up to him. He said it kept him sane, hearing things about home and her classes and his mom.

She went to see his mom every other weekend and really enjoyed those visits. They usually talked about Danny, comparing letters, wondering when he could come home, but they did other things too. Ginny may have never been thrilled about her childhood spent on farms, but she did know a thing or two about growing things. The soil and climate in Bakersfield were a farmer's dream, and with Ginny's help Mrs. Armbruster's Victory Garden was the best in the city.

Often, she and the girls from the boarding house would take a day trip to the beach to have a picnic and swim. Sometimes a few boys from the college would come along, too. They formed a little gang, and they went to movies and dances together. A few times she had gone out, one on one, with a couple of the boys, but she never felt comfortable with that.

She and Danny had made no promises. She had only known him for a few days before he shipped out. He was just a nice boy that helped the new kid in town. But as they wrote, she felt like she was really getting to know him. She couldn't bring herself to write to him that she had dates with anyone else, so it made her feel dishonest to go out at all. Maybe it was silly. The truth was she didn't need any complications anyway. She remembered well how few choices women get in life and she was hanging on to her choices.

Danny should have been home by now. Most soldiers had come back by the end of last year, but Danny was in the South Pacific and was probably going to be there until his military discharge. When he came home, he would be free of the Army. He never intended to be career military; he had enlisted to do his part. Fortunately, he had a talent for mechanical things and had been trained as an airplane mechanic. It was likely that he would continue in the field when he came home.

Ginny wrote to Chet nearly every week but, as expected, she was lucky if she got a scrawled note from him once a month. It sounded like he was doing ok. Almost as soon as they had moved to the farm, the forty acres adjoining JT's property had gone up for sale. The price was low, and Chet had always been good with money. He had a good chunk to put down. He somehow sweet-talked the local bank into a loan big enough to pay the balance of the property price plus enough to stock it with cattle. He was nearly at the end of the second year on the loan and assured her when he sold his calves off, he would have the annual payment. Ginny never told him, but she saved her money, too, and if it looked like he would have been in any danger of losing that property, she would have helped him out. She knew how much it meant to him to be able to build a cabin and get out of JT's house. She remembered what it was like to get her freedom, and she wanted that for Chet

# 8

## Chet and Greta

Soon after the rodeo, school started back up and that meant the Reddington kids had to get cows milked, chickens fed, and chores done before they washed and put on school clothes and ate breakfast. They envied Bill for not having to go to school anymore and he gloated, but secretly he missed going. It was a break from the farm that he rarely got anymore.

Greta did get some celebrity from being seen with Chet, but soon the hateful girls started sniggering behind their hands that there was only *one* reason a boy like Chet would be hanging around a farm girl like Greta. Greta knew they were jealous, and she knew very well that she and Chet hadn't done half of what she heard the other girls got up to, but it still hurt her feelings. She hated school. She always tried her best but most of the classes didn't seem important to her life. She did well in home-ec, and she liked to read so now that English class was mostly reading books, she did ok there, but mostly it just felt like a waste of time.

So, when in December Chet asked her if she wanted to get married, she was more than happy to leave school in the middle of her junior year. Ma and Daddy had warmed up to Chet right fine and if Chet's mother and stepfather weren't as friendly, they didn't seem unhappy with Greta. Chet had spent the fall working on that shack of his every chance he got. When he got the idea that he wasn't building it just for himself, he started working on making it a little more of a cabin than a shack, hoping maybe Greta would be able to make a home there. It came together faster with Bill's help and Chet was grateful to him.

Greta started making dish towels and curtains out of any flour sacks or other fabric she could find. When she picked apples in the fall, she saved the money and bought a whole bolt of muslin to make bed sheets. Ma was always making crazy quilts out of left-over scraps, and she let Greta add a couple of those to her "hope chest". As far as the hope chest itself went, Bill and Daddy had surprised her at Christmas with a cedar trunk that they had made themselves from trees cut off the farm. Everyone had seen where this was going and so no one was surprised when Chet bought a ring and made it official in December.

They were married in January at the County Courthouse. Ma went with them as a witness, but they didn't want any fuss or expense. The one thing that they spent a little extra on was having a portrait made at the photographer's studio. It was something they would always cherish.

Of course, mean girls will always be mean girls, so when Greta left school in January to start her new life as a Rancher's wife, rumors soon made it back to her about how she *had* to get married. That embarrassed her as much as it infuriated her. She was *not* that kind of girl.

Chet had made their little cabin as comfortable as he could. It had two good-sized rooms, a kitchen and a sitting room, with their full-sized bed in the corner. She and Ma found an old screen out in the barn and Ma helped her cover it with burlap from feed sacks, so that she had a little privacy for washing or could hide the bed if company came over. There was a wood stove in the sitting room that kept both rooms warm. Chet had built the chimney flue right in the center between the two rooms, so the stove sat in the middle of the house.

It was the kitchen that Greta loved! Chet had built her cabinets and countertops all along one wall with a dry sink right under the window. No running water in the house yet, but a drain ran from the sink to the garden outside. No more carrying out the dishpans to dump! Chet's sister had sent money for a wedding gift with the instructions to buy something pretty for the house. They had gone together and picked out a set of dark brown pottery plates and bowls and coffee mugs. The set was just for four, but the store said they could add pieces one at a time. Plates and bowls that all matched and no chips or scratches! Greta was so afraid to chip one that she kept using the hand-me-downs her mother had given her until Chet complained. "We bought those to use, Greta, not to save." Whenever he wasn't around, she was still likely to use an old coffee cup though.

And the *stove*. Chet had got her an almost new gas cookstove! And on top of that? A propane refrigerator! He got them together for a good price and said he thought he could afford a little propane if it kept the meat from spoiling.

Speaking of meat, being a beef rancher, Chet expected meat with every meal. At home they ate bacon or sausage pretty regular with breakfast and Daddy had hams in the smokehouse, but they ate little beef. Another thing that had confused her was when he brought home a fifty-pound bag of macaroni (he had traded for it somewhere) and plunked it on the kitchen table.

"What am I supposed to do with that?"

"Cook it and eat it was what I was thinking."

Greta was glad she had kept her old home-ec cookbook. She found a section on *pasta* and saw a few ways to cook macaroni. One was with tomatoes, and it looked good, but the one with cheese looked really good. Since Ma kept them supplied in milk and cheese from the dairy it was a dish she could make pretty often. She was so pleased when Chet liked it. She was learning a lot in her new life.

Most of Greta's days were spent cooking and cleaning and trying to make a yard out of the field the house was in. Chet's days were taking care of farm chores and trading whatever he could in town to make a little extra cash. Sometimes he would get paid to haul a load of heavy household goods to the dump and if he sorted through, he could often find a piece of furniture that could be repaired or some old iron that could be sold at the scrap yard. Since he wasn't eating his meals with Mother and JT anymore, JT couldn't hold him to being his unpaid farm hand and that gave him more time for himself, though his mother still found ways to get him to help JT out some.

They would eat dinner on Sunday afternoon at Chet's folks' house and once or twice a month supper with Greta's family. Greta would like to have spent more time with her folks, but they could walk to Chet's mother's house, and it was a drive to her family's place. She kind of missed those rowdy little brothers, though. Truth was, Chet wished his place was closer to the Reddington's and further from the Smith's, but the deal on the place had been good and it seemed like a great idea when he was fifteen, to have the property close so he could work it while living at home. Not much way to change it now.

Winter passed to spring and Greta worked her fingers to the bone trying to get a vegetable garden to grow as well as planting flowers and rose bushes that she got from starts that she brought from her Ma's plants. Nothing seemed to grow as well for her as it did for Ma.

Summer came on and with it the news from Greta that she and Chet were expecting their first baby. Both sets of grandparents were delighted, and Chet was tickled, but a little worried about the expense. He knew when they got married that this was inevitable, but he had hoped it would take a bit longer. So now when he gathered junk to haul, he kept an eye open for cribs and highchairs.

# 9

# Alton

When their son was born the following March, he was perfect and healthy and surrounded with love. Except for the argument over his name. Greta wanted a little boy named after his father. The problem was Chet hated his given name. Alfred Chester Masters. Gawd. Only someone like Mother would hang a handle like that on a kid. Fortunately, the plan had been to call him Chester and Ginny, who had been just learning to talk well herself, couldn't say it. She called him "Chet" and it sort of stuck. So as far as Chet was concerned Ginny named him and that was ok with him.

Greta didn't think Chet was a "real" name and besides it would be confusing. If they called him Chet Junior, pretty soon it would just be Junior. Nope. Not having that.

Chet suggested James.

"Why James?"

"Well," Chet looked at his feet and mumbled, "JT's name is James Thomas."

Greta was almost horrified. "Are you kidding me? You want to name our sweet little boy after a man you practically hate?!"

"I never said I hated him."

"No, sorry. I think you said, 'you can't stand him.' I see the difference."

"Now, settle down..."

"What did you just say to me?"

Uhoh. Chet knew that look. He had spent enough time around Greta, Bill and the other Reddington's to know that look meant a storm was brewing.

"I just mean we can talk it over. He may not be a perfect man or even a good one, but he is the only father I ever knew."

Greta's look changed immediately from angry to confused. It wasn't like Chet to be sentimental. When she said, "I love you" the best she got was "me too". This must mean more to him than he was letting on.

"But if we name him James, he will get called Jimmy like a hundred other Jimmy's within rock throwing distance."

"We don't have to call him that. We can give him another name."

"Ok, that's fair I suppose. My Daddy's middle name is Alton."

"Earl Alton Reddington? His mama had high hopes for him, didn't she?"

"The Reddington's are an old family I'll have you know. Came over in colonial times. Those are family names."

"Well, Alton is a fine name I suppose."

"James Alton?"

"Sounds good. We'll call him Al?"

Greta sighed. "I suppose it's inevitable but maybe we can call him Alton enough that he knows it's his name."

At that moment, the young child in question made a mewling noise from his bassinet. Chet walked over and looked down at his son. "Hello James Alton. How does that suit you?" Alton cooed and they heard a rumbling noise from his diaper.

"It seems like he doesn't mind it too much," Chet laughed as he stepped away to let Greta scoop Alton up to change him and feed him.

As the days went by, Greta nursed Alton every time he was interested but it seemed he was hungry all the time. Doctor Jeffries, Starkville's only doctor, saw Alton at two weeks old.

"You were right to bring him to me, Greta. He isn't thriving. How often do you feed him?"

"As often as he wants. I feel like I've done nothing else."

"You do look tired. Greta, nursing him yourself may not be right for you. Your baby might do better on a baby formula. You can make your own with evaporated milk and corn syrup or there are some versions available to buy."

"Not feed him myself? I can do better. I'll eat better"

"Greta, it's not you. It may be that the baby just can't break down the milk. Some babies just don't. And we used to lose those babies, Greta. We are lucky to live in a time when we know how to feed a baby with formula."

That did make Greta feel better, but she was still disappointed. She carried Alton out to the truck where Chet was waiting. She had the card with instructions for formula in her hand.

"Doctor says I can't feed him right. He needs formula"

"What does that even mean? You've been feeding him!"

"I know, but it's not enough. Chet he was serious. He said he could die."

"Well then we get what we need."

"We are going to need bottles with rings, nipples and caps. A brush to wash them. A sterilizer or a large pot if it has something to keep the bottles off the bottom."

"Like a canner?"

"Yeah, but it doesn't need to be that big."

"I think I have an idea. What else?"

"Karo syrup and evaporated milk."

"We can't use regular milk?"

"He said follow the directions *exactly*. Changing anything could hurt him."

"Ok, ok." Let's go buy what we need. I think Mother has the pot that will work."

They bought 8 bottles and the milk and syrup. On the way home they stopped and told his mother and JT what the doctor said.

"Oh, you poor thing, come to Grandmother," was his mother's response before she pulled Alton from Greta's arms. She shot Greta a look like she had been abusing him, which did nothing to settle Greta's nerves. She had given birth in Doctor Jeffries office two weeks ago and Chet had brought her home as soon as she was fit to ride in the truck. Her Ma had told her to stay in bed as much as she could for the first six weeks and Doctor Jeffries had agreed. But with a baby that wanted to eat all the time, she felt like she hadn't slept a wink in two weeks. And today had been another bumpy truck ride, the doctor, the store ... Greta was about at her limit and that old crone looking down her nose at her was past the limit!

Once again, Chet saw that look and headed off the storm. "You come sit down, darlin'. Take the soft chair and put your feet up. We can look for a pot that will work, while you rest a bit."

"Thank you, Chet, I am tired." He tucked Alton in beside her on the chair. In about two minutes she was asleep.

"Poor thing. She's been run off her feet, hasn't she?"

Chet was totally exasperated with his mother. "Why can't you ever say anything that nice when she can hear you?"

Mother turned away, "I don't know what you're talking about."

"You never do", Chet muttered under his breath.

Chet thought his mother's pressure cooker would be just the thing. It had a wire basket, and it would hold all eight bottles. What he hadn't figured out was how tall the bottles were. The lid wouldn't go on.

"Let me think a minute." His mother went to the deepwell in her kitchen stove. It was a kind of slow cooker built into the stove top. She reached in and pulled out the pan. The pan was like a stock pot but since it was made to fit inside the well it didn't have handles that would get in the way. She sat it down over the pressure cooker full of bottles and it slid in place like it was made for it. Maybe too well. She cautioned Chet. "It doesn't have a place for air to escape so you may need to prop a butter knife under the edge, so it doesn't build up pressure. But I think it will work.

Chet looked it over. It looked almost like the sterilizer in the store, except as Mother pointed out, the one in the store had a steam hole on top. This would work.

"Thank you, Mother."

"Chet, I'd do anything for that little boy. This is nothing."

For possibly the first time in his life Chet felt like he had done something his mother could be proud of. She really loved that baby.

He put the pot and all the bottles back in the truck and woke Greta. "Let's get the two of you home."

"Sounds good to me."

It was a half mile from one house to the other, so it was a short ride. Greta took Alton in and nursed him one more time before she put him down again.

While she was nursing, Chet had gone for a bucket of well water. He put it on the stove to heat. As soon as she had Alton down, she headed to the kitchen. She started pulling out measuring cups and spoons and a big pitcher to mix in.

"Darlin' lay down, I can do this."

"Chet, I'm tired, and I would surely love some help, but I have to mix it myself. Doctor Jeffries told me how bad it could be if we don't follow the recipe. I have to see it with my own eyes, or I'd be scared to feed him."

"Ok, we will do it together". Chet looked at Greta, at how worn out she was, and how stubborn she was. She was just a tiny little thing, barely more than a girl herself and she was trying so hard to do everything on her own. He remembered the feeling, the first time he ever saw her, and thought 'lovely' was the word that described her best. He still did. As she stood there, tired to the bone, her hair a tangled mess and not a scrap of make-up she was just lovely. If only he knew how to say that.

"Just tell me what to do."

"If that water is hot, wash those bottles. Warm soapy water and use the brush we bought to reach the bottom. Wash the nipples, caps and rings and force water through the nipples to make sure they work." While Chet set to work Greta carefully measured canned milk, syrup and water into the big pitcher and stirred until the syrup was completely dissolved and she was satisfied that all was mixed. As Chet handed her clean bottles, she filled them and loosely put on caps with nipples hanging down inside.

"Why do you put them together upside down?"

"It keeps them clean until you are ready then you flip them right way up."

"Is there still warm water in the bucket? Not hot, just warm?"

"Yeah."

She set all the bottles down carefully in the pot. "Ok, pour water in, about half full".

They set it on the stove and put the lid on, cocked a little to the side to let steam out. Then they lit the burner under it.

Chet stood back a step. "What now?"

"Well now we wait for it to boil, turn it down and let it simmer for forty-five minutes, turn it off, let it cool, tighten the caps and put them away in the refrigerator. Don't let it boil dry or we'll have a mess."

"It is like canning. Do we do this every day?"

Greta laughed, "I hope not! It should be enough to last a few days."

"Oh, that's good. But I can watch this. You go to bed now."

Greta looked at the bed longingly. "Are you sure?"

"Of course, I'm sure. I'll have to go feed cows in a bit, but I can watch this first."

Greta needed no more persuasion. She was ready for a nap. A good long one if she could get it.

When Greta woke next, it was to the smell of bacon. She reached for Alton and his bassinet wasn't there. She sat up sharply and looked around the room. Through the door to the kitchen, she could see the bassinet near the counter. One the counter was a neat row of baby bottles, cooling. She counted 7. Oh no, did one break?

She got out of bed and went to the kitchen. Chet was frying bacon in one skillet and potatoes in another. The sterilizer pot was by the sink, draining. There was bread, spread with mayo and thick slices of cheddar laying on the cutting board. Alton was asleep on his tummy looking more peaceful than she had ever seen him.

She had so many questions she didn't know where to start. Start with the baby. "Why is Alton in here?"

"Oh, hello sleepy head. I was fixin' to wake you up. When I came back from feeding' the cows he was fussin' pretty good, and you hadn't woke up. The bottles was coolin', I put one in cool water to cool it faster while I changed him and fed him and then I brought his cot in here so we wouldn't bother you. But you were out, so I don't think we could have bothered you."

"I can't believe I slept through him cryin', oh Chet I'm so sorry!"

"Sorry?! Well, honey you didn't do nuthin' wrong! Your poor little body is just tuckered out. I'm sorry I didn't see it sooner. If a cow was having that much trouble feedin' a calf, I'd a been bottle feedin' that calf to give her a break, but I didn't know what to look for with a baby."

"Aw Chet, you're a good man. But I'm supposed to take care of the house and the baby. You have man's work to do."

Chet took the bacon out of the frying pan and put it on some brown paper to drain. He turned the heat down under the potatoes and put a lid on them. Then he walked over to Greta and put his arms around her. "Darlin' what you say is true. Most times, I'd be out workin' to keep us in money, and I'd expect you to keep up your side. But we are a team. I might get sick sometime, and you would need to feed cows for me."

"But that ain't the same..."

"How is it not the same darlin'?"

"You're not supposed to do the cookin'. And that's another question; you can cook?"

Chet threw his head back and laughed. "Well, hell darlin' a man has to eat! I been out on hunts with my uncles, and we all took turns cookin'. Granny Masters didn't always feel like cookin' so she taught me how. I had expected to live in this house by myself if I hadn't met you. I would have had to feed myself somehow."

"I just can't imagine Daddy or Bill cookin' anything. I think they would starve if Ma didn't feed em."

"Yeah, I think that's what they want you to believe. Now. You been standin' there too long. Go sit yourself down and let me get this supper finished.

She sat down at the table and pulled Alton's bassinet closer to the table. "I've never seen him sleep so well."

"He drank a couple of ounces, burped a big ol' burp and was conked before I had him tucked. I put him on his belly in case he spit up, but he hasn't wiggled at all."

"Well, guess he likes the formula. I don't know how I feel about that."

"Sugar, you are just happy that he's happy. That's all."

"Yeah, of course. I know that. I just wish I could nurse him. But hey, I just realized! You fed him! Oh my. Maybe I do like this bottle thing!"

"There's my girl! Lookin' on the bright side." He pushed a plate in front of her with a sandwich, thick with bacon and cheese, crispy fried potatoes, and opened a bottle of Coke and set it by her plate. "Now you eat."

"Where did we get Coke?"

"Mother sent a couple home with us. She is a believer that a Coke now and then will cure what ails ya."

"I'm not sure I believe that, but I appreciate the treat. And I appreciate you! I sure was smart, gettin' you to marry me!"

"You sure were!"

# 10

# Furnishings

In September, Ginny was in her apartment. It was small, but it was a one-bedroom, not a studio, and she loved it. She was collecting furniture one piece at a time. She wanted good things. Used was ok, but she wanted good quality, and modern-looking furniture. So, she was picky. She did have a nice single-size bed and a nightstand which was about all her bedroom would hold. Maybe a small chair if she saw the right one.

The living room was empty. She had a small table and two chairs that would never have fit in her galley kitchen, sitting close to the kitchen door. There was a lamp on a packing crate near the front door but that was it, so far. She had everything that she needed to cook simple meals in her kitchen, and she enjoyed cooking and washing and putting things away in her very own kitchen.

Danny was home. His mother had been keeping him close by her side for the two weeks he had been back, and Danny was cheerfully letting her have that. She had held her breath for two years waiting for him to come back safely. He had been by Ginny's apartment to bring a housewarming present from his mother. It was a potted plant in a beautiful Mexican terra cotta pot. It looked lovely by the living room window.

He had looked around her empty room while she explained she was looking for just the right pieces. He told her he had a friend that ran a little used furniture store just outside of town. He offered to drive her out to look through his inventory this coming weekend. She told him she didn't have much of a budget, but he said it wouldn't hurt to look. She had asked him if he would have time to stay for dinner afterward, and he had agreed. So, she had a couple of days to figure out a meal that wouldn't take much time to cook but would seem special.

On Saturday, Danny knocked on her door promptly at one o'clock. She had made herself a quick lunch and had just finished up clearing her dishes and putting chicken pieces in the refrigerator to marinate. She had decided that it would be easy to throw that in the oven when they got back from furniture shopping, and she could throw a couple of potatoes in at the same time. She wiped her hands, took off her apron and skipped to the door.

Ginny opened the door to Danny with his arms full of garden vegetables. "Mom sent you a few things."

"I can see that! The garden is doing well, then?"

"Oh, yes. Mom has had me pulling weeds and watering and picking. I think you created a monster."

"It wasn't my doing, I just helped her out. I think she has really enjoyed her new hobby though."

"I'm just not sure how much *I* enjoy her new hobby."

"Well let's get this stowed away so we can get going."

Ginny grabbed her handbag as they stepped out the door, and as she was locking up, Danny opened the passenger door of his mom's old Buick for her to climb in. Ginny settled in as Danny climbed in and started the motor. "I like this car. It's so comfortable."

"Yes, Mom hardly ever drives. It's like new. I wonder why she keeps it."

"Oh, I understand. She just likes knowing that she can go when she wants to. It's freedom"

"I guess I never looked at it like that. She doesn't go much of anywhere further than walking distance."

"Yes, but she knows she could. It's nice to be able to, even if you never want to.

"Hmmmm.'

It was only about a twenty-minute drive to the shop that was owned by Danny's friend. They pulled off of the highway into a gravel parking area. There was a large showroom window with some beautiful furniture displayed. It was low and modern, just what she wanted. It was all there, down to lamps and ashtrays. It looked expensive. Danny read Ginny's expression and knew what she was thinking. "Don't worry, he shows the best up front, but he has things for every budget. And I let him know we were coming today; he is expecting us." They walked in through the front entrance as Danny's friend, Ted, walked in from the back room. "Dan! It's great to see you! He crossed the showroom in three leggy strides and was shaking Dan's hand and patting him on the shoulder. "You look good, really good!"

"You look good too, Ted. It's great to see you! This is Ginny. Ginny, this is Ted Moncrief. We went to grade school together."

"Friends since day one, grade one," Ted said as he turned to look at Ginny. She held out her hand for a quick shake and Ted winked at Danny, "You didn't tell me what a looker she is. Blue eyes and dark brown hair. Wowie! I dream of Ginny!"

"I may not have mentioned Ginny; Ted can be a tad enthusiastic."

"I see."

"Not at all, just brutally honest. Now Ginny, Danny says you're broke and need furniture..."

Well, I wouldn't say I was ..."

"Ted! You know I said no such thing!" Danny turned to look at Ginny, the blush creeping from his collar to his forehead. "Ginny, I just told him we wanted to look and see what he had. Honestly."

"Yeah. I may have inferred the rest." "C'mon let's head out back."

Ginny nodded to Danny, and they followed Ted, who moved faster than anyone Ginny had ever seen, so she had a chance to reassure Danny, "Don't worry, I like him. He just says what he thinks. At least you know where he stands."

"Oh, that you do. He won't keep you in suspense. Just don't tell him your deep dark secrets. He couldn't keep a secret if he tried."

"I'll try not to have any deep dark secrets, then."

They arrived in the room behind the showroom. It was a large open area, split about in half as workshop and warehouse. "I take in a lot of furniture on trade and sometimes I buy whole households as people are moving. I can fix things up, paint or varnish, sometimes do simple upholstery. It keeps me in showy things for the front room and helps keep my prices down.

"Well, Ted, I think you're smart. Is the furniture in the front window new?"

"It is now! Nah, that's a set I took in a while back. It was in good shape with just a few nicks and scratches. I sanded and was able to match the stain so now it is as good as new. I've got it priced at nearly half of what it was when it was new though."

"Very smart." Ginny started to walk through the rows of furniture on the warehouse side. "You know, Ted, I have several girlfriends who are just getting their first apartments. Quite a few of us graduated last May from secretarial school and several more will next May. As they get jobs they are getting their own places. I could probably refer you a lot of business."

"I do like the way you think. And suppose when one of these referrals came in, I gave you ten per cent of their sale towards your purchases?"

"I suppose I'd like that right fine."

Danny just stepped back and watched the two of them. It seemed like he had done his part here. Ginny was holding her own with Ted.

"So, Ginny, what kind of furniture are you looking for?"

"I like modern styles. I'm sick of the stuffy Victorian things I grew up with."

"I hear ya. What did you think of the set in the window?"

"I think even at half of the original price it's more than I could afford. I was thinking maybe just a chair and coffee table for now and I'll add pieces as I can."

"I understand. But what if I told you, that you could pay for the chair and the coffee table today and have the whole set now and just pay as you go, how would that be?"

"Oh, I don't know. I don't usually like to owe anyone. How much interest would you charge?"

"I wasn't thinking of charging you interest."

"Then how could you afford to wait for payment?"

"Well Ginny, I got that whole living room set really cheap, lamps, tables and all. I told you; it was just a few scratches to fix it up. Danny says you have a good job, you could just pay me a little from each paycheck. And remember, I'm going to give you money off your purchase every time one of your friends buys something from me. And don't worry, I'm going to give them all good deals, too."

"I'm still a little worried about owing money. What if my job didn't work out?"

"I'm not worried about that, but just for the sake of 'what ifs' let's say you couldn't pay it all off. Well, we would just figure out how much was paid for, and I'd pick up the rest to sell again."

"I suppose that's fair enough."

It went against everything that Ginny had ever been taught to owe money for purchases. She was raised to only buy what you could afford and even then, make sure you were saving against an emergency. When her mother had been left with nothing it had left an impression, one that was reinforced by years of scrimping and saving. Sure, Chet got loans for cattle and property, but this wasn't business. This was just furniture. But, oh, how she wanted that furniture. Her apartment would look like a magazine. She just couldn't resist.

She looked at Danny. "What do you think, Danny?"

"I think it's up to you. You have a good job. If Ted says he can work with you then he will. But the decision is yours."

The decision was hers. Wasn't that why she was even in California? To make her own decisions? Mother and JT had always told her, "Ask yourself before every purchase, 'do I *need* it?'" The answer was no, she didn't *need* it. But she *wanted* it!

"Ted, if you can give me time to pay for all of it, then yes, let's go look at the furniture in the window.

In the end she didn't take everything from the window. She let Ted keep the ashtray, even though it looked gorgeous on the coffee table. But one habit she abhorred was smoking. It was so popular with most of the people she knew. Even at her office she was to keep cigarette boxes and lighters full for the client's convenience. But raised on the farm, none of the grandparents smoked and Mother and JT never did. She hated the way it smelled. Her house was going to smell of fresh flowers, not smoke. Oddly enough, she just realized she had never seen Danny smoke. As she was telling Ted she wouldn't need the ashtray, she paused and glanced at Danny. "Do you ever smoke?"

"No, I was the only one in my platoon who didn't, too, I just can't stand the smell.

Huh. One more thing they had in common.

Anyway, with the final deal she had a small low sofa, a convertible type where the back would fold flat and make it into a bed. It had wooden armrests and yellow upholstered cushions, very square and neat. There were two chairs to match, a small coffee table and two end tables. The lamps were yellow and sort of red/orange that complemented the upholstery. There was a high console table, meant to sit behind the couch in a large room, but in her space, it would go by the front door to hold her lamp. No more crate!

Danny helped Ted load everything on his truck and he said he would be by with it this evening, right after he closed the shop. Ginny was so excited. She had never made such a big purchase, and it would all be in her apartment tonight!

Since there was time to kill before she started dinner, she and Danny stopped at a store that sold fabric by the yard and she picked out just what she wanted for curtains and a tablecloth. It was a cheery yellow background with thin red and orange triangles and squares. But she would not let herself buy it today. She had spent all that she had budgeted for today on the downpayment and taken on debt besides. She wouldn't buy more today. And, as she told Danny, she needed to measure the window anyway.

When she and Danny got back to her apartment, she told him to have a seat at the table, currently the only place to sit, and she went to the kitchen to pop the chicken and potatoes in the oven. When she came out of the kitchen, a tray of cheese and crackers in one hand and two Cokes in the other, she found Danny, measuring tape in hand, kneeling in front of the window in the living room.

"What *are* you doing?"

Danny jotted a couple of numbers down on the pad he kept in his shirt pocket. "You mentioned needing to measure the window and Mom had a tape measure in the toolbox in the Buick, so I just thought I would jot some numbers down."

"Well, thank you for that. Would you like some nibbles before dinner? And a Coke?

"Oh, yes please." He pulled his keyring from his pocket and used the church-key key fob to open the Cokes. "Mmmmm, ice cold, just the way I like it."

"You know, my mother swears that a Coke every once in a while, will cure what ails you.'

"I think she may be right."

"I suppose she would have to be right sometimes."

Danny let that go. He was wise enough not to ask too many questions when it came to girls and their mothers. Touchy subject.

# 11

# Choices

September of the following year, Ginny had settled into a routine and was quite happy with her life. Her job was going well, and she found the work interesting. Her boss was a nice man and a very successful attorney, and he saw right away that Ginny was a valuable asset. She was never afraid to speak up. When dictating a letter, soon after she started working for him, he was surprised when she interrupted to suggest he change the phrasing of a line, and was about to put her in her place, when he realized she was right. Over the next few letters, she never said a word, but then, eventually, she suggested a correction and again he realized that she was right. In his line of work, the phrasing of a sentence was very important, and he was impressed that she spoke up, but only when necessary. He soon had her going over contracts looking for ways to improve the wording, and often she was able to make suggestions that did indeed clarify the intent of the document.

He asked her one time how she came to have such a grasp of language and particularly the nuances that could be misunderstood. He knew several graduates from her background at Bakersfield College and he didn't think that was where she got her education.

"I guess I have to give my mother credit there, sir," she replied after giving the matter some thought. "I was reading by age three and have always been a voracious reader. Mother is a teacher, so when we discussed books, I was reading, she would have me present the material in different ways. I guess that stuck." She tapped her chin thoughtfully with her pencil while she pondered that for a moment.

"She sounds like a wonderful woman."

That brought Ginny out of her reverie. "An interesting woman, yes. I can say that honestly."

Ginny was never bored at work, as so many of her girlfriends complained. She loved her job and her little apartment. She was wondering if she could get Chet out here for a visit this fall. She would love for him to meet Danny.

She and Danny saw each other frequently. A few days after her furniture had arrived for her living room, Danny had shown up on her doorstep carrying yards and yards of the fabric that she had chosen for curtains.

"Danny, I told you I need to wait awhile before spending any more on the apartment!"

"I know, that's why I bought all this." It's my housewarming gift to you."

"But you and your mother already gave me the lovely potted plant"

"That was from Mom. I was strictly the delivery boy."

"But Danny, this is too much."

"Ginny, it's not. I plan on spending a good deal of time in this room. I want it to look nice!' He grinned and she found it hard to argue.

That weekend when he came to pick her up for a movie, he saw that she was sewing her curtains all by hand.

"It never occurred to me; you don't have a sewing machine, do you?"

"Well, no. I don't sew all that often. I do most everything by hand."

So, after much arguing, and Ginny's eventual capitulation, Danny came by on Sunday to pick up Ginny and all her material and she and Mom Armbruster made her curtains, tablecloth, and with material left over they made small placemats that could be scattered on end tables to add bright pops of color.

She was so proud of her apartment. Her furniture was paid off. Her deal with Ted had proved quite lucrative. So many of her friends bought furniture from him that she hadn't ever had to pay another dime to her debt. Two friends had married and moved into larger houses, and Ted was the furniture man to them all. His little store was expanding, and he had two employees help him now, to keep up with all the sales.

Danny had partnered with a friend who was also an airplane mechanic, and they had opened a small shop in a rented hangar at the airfield. They were also doing well. They worked on small passenger planes, but a great deal of their business came from crop-dusters.

It seemed like the hard years of the depression, and then the war, had finally passed. She was feeling sure it was time to get Chet out for a visit, when she got one of her rare letters from him. This one was indeed rare, it covered two pages, front and back. He told her about paying off his place, starting work on his house with a new friend named Bill, about how he had gone to the rodeo on Smoke, oh, and that Bill had a sister named Greta. He had actually met Greta first and then they all went to the rodeo together. He mentioned Greta, quite casually, a few times in that letter. Chet had never written to her about any girl before. He might say, 'I took a date to see that Western' or some kind of thing but never all about one girl. Ginny thought maybe this wasn't the right time to invite Chet out after all.

A few more letters came over the fall, with lots of stories about Bill and his sister Greta. When the letter came in December saying he had asked Greta to marry him, she wasn't surprised at all. He had his little cabin ready, and they were to be married next month. Good for Chet. Ginny wished him well. She sent them a small gift and a pretty large money order with instructions for Chet to buy Greta something pretty for their home.

In mid-December, Danny was at Ginny's apartment helping her decorate a Christmas tree. She thought it was a little silly to bother but Danny wouldn't hear of her not having a tree. They settled on a small one and her potted plant was ousted from its familiar spot by the window to give the tree a place of honor.

Ginny had gone to the kitchen to make them both a cup of warm cider to sip with the Christmas cookies. She walked back into the living room with a tray that she placed on the coffee table. Danny was on his knees by the tree.

"What are you doing there, I thought we were done with the tree?"

"I want you to look, there is something sparkly I want you to see." Ginny walked near him and started to bend down when he grabbed her left hand. "See how that sparkles in the light?", he said as he pushed a ring onto her finger. "Ginny, I want you to marry me."

Ginny gasped! It was not that it was totally unexpected, she knew how they felt about each other. She knew that even before he had come back to Bakersfield but in the last year and a half, they had been inseparable. She loved Danny, she truly did, but marriage was a scary thing for her. In her experience when a girl made the choice to marry, her choices from then on weren't her own. Was she ready for that?

Danny led her to the couch. "Ginny, I've known you for a good while now. You don't talk about your family much, except for Chet, but I've been able to piece a thing or two together, Ginny, it would be different for us. I would never try to take away your independence. It's what I love about you."

"I know Danny and I trust you. But the world doesn't give women the advantages it gives men. I work for an *attorney*. I'm educated and live on my own. But I couldn't open a bank account to put my paycheck in because I don't have a male relative to sign for me. My boss has to write me checks, then cash them for me to give me my money. It's embarrassing. I can't invest my money; I just have to hide it in the cookie jar. I just couldn't bear to give away any of the freedoms I do have."

"Ginny, look at it this way. If you trust me, and I hope you do, I could be a help to you. It isn't right that a sentient female in the modern age can go to college, go to work but make less and not be able to cash her own paycheck. It's wrong Ginny. But I could help you. We could open accounts for you, but they would be just yours. I would never take anything from you. I could sign for you to make investments, but I would never tell you what you could or couldn't invest in. I just couldn't Ginny. The day I saw you trying to drag your luggage by yourself rather than ask for help, I knew who you were. Anyone else getting off the bus in unknown territory would have been scared to death, but you looked like you were here to conquer the world. I love you, Ginny. I would never change you."

In the end Ginny knew what her choice would be. It really wasn't a choice at all. "Yes, Danny, how soon can we be married?

~~~

Even though once the decision was made, Ginny would have married Danny the next day, as it turned out, she was the one who wanted to wait a while. Chet had just proposed to his girl, and they were getting married in January. Ginny didn't want to steal their thunder, so she didn't want to announce their engagement yet. That didn't mean they couldn't tell Danny's mom though. They headed straight over to see her.

As they walked into the Armbruster home, Mom took one look at them holding hands and smiling and said, "So, you're getting married."

"Gee Mom, talk about spoiling the surprise!"

"Oh, a surprise, is it? When you spend more time together than you do apart? Surprise. The surprise is how long you've waited."

Mom muttered all this as she walked toward the kitchen. Danny shrugged at Ginny, and they followed. On the table was a tray with three tall glasses, small plates, forks and napkins. She reached into the refrigerator and pulled out a bottle of Champagne and added it to the tray. "Daniel, carry this through to the dining room." She handed Ginny a bowl of fresh strawberries. "You follow him, dearie."
~~~

She reached back into the refrigerator one more time and came out with a cake that was decorated with white roses and said 'Congratulations' in silver icing.

In the dining room, silver paper wedding bells were hanging from the chandelier over the dining table. Mom put the cake down on the table near the tray and strawberries. She stood back with a very satisfied smile.

"MOM! When did you do all this?

"Oh, when will children learn? You can't hide anything from me. I knew when you bought the ring, and I saw you put it in your pocket before you left. Now, if she had said 'no' I would have been in a pickle, but I didn't expect she would.

"Mom Armbruster, you are a character."

"It's just 'Mom' now, don't you think dearie?"

"Yes, Mom, I think it's fine."

# 12

# The Masters'

After starting on formula, Alton made up for lost time and started growing by leaps and bounds. He soon outgrew his little bassinet and Chet brought in a crib for him, that they put right at the foot of their bed. Chet had found a little chest of drawers and Greta had cleaned and painted it so they had a place to store Alton's clothes and diapers. But soon the baby had taken over the house. Greta tried to keep his things picked up, but as soon as he started crawling, he was everywhere, and his things were everywhere.

Chet came in from feeding the cows and saw Greta in the middle of the chaos, looking like she was going to cry.

"I've been trying to get this picked up, but I needed to get dinner started and he pulled over the whole stack of laundry and...."

"Greta, it's ok. I can help fold the laundry back up. But the bigger problem here is we need another room. You can't put stuff away if there's nowhere to put it and we can't fit any more furniture in this room."

"Well, how are we gonna get another room?"

"I reckon Bill and I are going to have to build one. That's all we can do."

"How can we pay for that?"

"It won't be that much; I've been working it out in my head for a while. Remember a month or so ago I used our tractor and pulled out those stumps for Dave Bishop? I didn't let him pay me, but I told him I might need his help sometime. If I build forms, he could come pour a slab for us and he gets the concrete cheaper and he won't charge us extra for it. For the rest of it, it's just lumber and hardware. I'll cut oak for the roof timbers myself. We can do it."

"You have been thinking about it! Oh Chet, it would be a wonder to have Alton in a space where he wasn't into everything. He's starting to pull up, he's gonna walk soon and I won't be able to keep up!" .

"I'll go see Dave after dinner. The slab is the hardest part, after that Bill and I can figure it out, just like we did with the rest of the house.

About two months later, the room was ready, and not a minute too soon. Alton had indeed started walking and was amazingly fast. How one little boy could wreak so much havoc was a mystery. Greta had practically raised her younger brothers, and she didn't remember them being this way. If she washed Alton's face and tucked his little shirt in, before she turned around, he was untucked, and his face was dirty. He would put *anything* in his mouth, including bugs. He was a little chubby legged tornado. "Good thing you're so cute", was something Greta said several times a day. She thought he was starting to understand, because he would often give her a little grin, showing all four teeth, whenever she said it.

The room wasn't huge, maybe ten feet by twelve feet but it seemed like it doubled the size of the house. As soon as Chet said it was ready to go, Greta started moving the crib toward the door.

"Are you sure you want to move his crib in there? He has never slept by himself."

"Oh. I'm sure. He's gonna learn how! But we can leave the door open. He can still see us."

Chet had done a very clever thing with the door. Since the whole idea was to have a place for Alton and all his stuff, Chet had made a split door. It could be opened as one piece, like a regular door or, by releasing a couple of latches, the bottom half could stay closed and the top half open. The bottom half was about thirty inches tall, so it was high enough to keep Alton inside, but Greta could still step over if she needed to. The plan was to not put anything in that room that wasn't Alton's. It was his domain.

Grandmother and 'Papa" JT had questioned why the baby got his own room while Chet and Greta would keep their bed in the living room. JT didn't think it was 'proper'. Greta just thought it was foolish to worry about how it looked, she needed that baby to be somewhere safe and out from under foot, at least part of the time.

Alton made quick work of looking in every corner. He crawled under his crib and sat up and clapped his hands together. "I think he likes it." Greta said. Chet nodded and smiled. It felt good to make things better for his family.

Alton had just passed his first birthday and still hadn't met his Aunt Ginny or Uncle Danny. In fact, no one had met Danny yet. In the first summer after Chet and Greta got married, fancy envelopes had arrived, one addressed to Mr. and Mrs. Chet Masters and one for Mr. and Mrs. JT Smith. The return address was Bakersfield but not Ginny's address. Chet's mother had picked up the mail and called them to come over. They all opened their envelopes together.

Beautifully hand lettered cards read:

*Mrs. Seraphina Armbruster*
*Is proud to announce*
*The upcoming marriage of*
*Her son,*
*Daniel Armbruster*
*To*
*Miss Virginia Masters*
*Small private ceremony*
*To be held*
*December 15, 1948*

Chet grinned ear to ear, "Well, I'll be."

Chet's mother checked the envelope to see if there was another page. She flipped the card over twice, and then said in the most bewildered way, "Why, it doesn't give a time or location for the ceremony. I don't understand."

"It's because it isn't an invitation," said JT as he went and plopped into his recliner.

"Well, of course it is. What else would it be?"

"It says 'announce' not 'invite'. I think that makes it an announcement." JT popped a toothpick in his mouth and leaned back in the recliner and closed his eyes. To him, the matter was settled.

"Why wouldn't Ginny want us there for her wedding, it makes no sense at all."

Chet spoke up, "Ginny didn't come to ours."

"Well, that was different, you got married at the courthouse. But this is Ginny. She will want her mother there."

"Maybe 'small private ceremony' is fancy talk for 'at the courthouse'."

"No. Ginny wouldn't plan out to get married at the courthouse. It's not proper."

"You didn't object to us getting married at the courthouse." Greta felt a sting from her mother-in-law's words.

"The hurry you two were in, we just suspected there was some reason you didn't want to wait for a church wedding." She raised an eyebrow and looked straight at Greta.

Greta gasped and took a step back. She blushed a deep red and was absolutely speechless.

Chet stepped in, "Here now. What cause do you have to say anything like that to my wife? I'm used to you talking to me like I was something you found stuck to the bottom of your shoe, but Greta has been nothing but sweet to you. And if a courthouse wedding was good enough for us, I suspect it will be good enough for Ginny and Danny!"

With that he put a hand on Greta's back and escorted her out the door. After they had walked about halfway home, Greta said, "I never knew your mother felt that way about me."

Chet put his arm around her shoulders and pulled her to him, "She doesn't have a thing in the world against you. She's mad at Ginny. Ginny was always a good girl, her grades were good, she didn't talk back, but the truth is, Mother never paid her any more attention than she did me. Less really, because I was always in trouble. Ever since Ginny went to California, Mother acts like she lost her best friend. She honestly can't imagine that Ginny doesn't care to have her at her wedding. And if I know Ginny, she isn't wasting money on a wedding when there is a marriage to be planning for."

Greta leaned against him, and she took comfort in his words, but she wasn't the type to forget. Mrs. Smith had made her feel as lousy as those back-biting girls in school used to and she started to see why Chet wasn't as close to his mother as she was to hers.

After the screen door slammed, JT said, "You made a mess of that."

His wife looked at him lying back in his recliner. He hadn't even opened his eyes. "Well, you weren't much help. Why aren't you upset about this? Our daughter doesn't want us at her wedding!"

At that JT opened his eyes. "She ain't my daughter. My daughter is in Starkville cemetery because you couldn't manage to get me a live child."

"That's low JT. And I'll remind you that I had two live children. It could be your fault, not mine."

"Be that as it may, *your daughter* has done us a favor. I'm not paying for a trip to California to watch your uppity offspring marry a grease monkey."

"He is an airplane mechanic, JT. It's a very specialized field."

"I'm just saying, girl goes to a fancy school so she can work for lawyers, but she doesn't nab one of them. She marries a grease monkey."

"JT, I regret the day I ever met you."

"Me too lady, me too."

After several letters and one long-distance phone call, Ginny finally had her mother convinced that they just didn't want to cause a bother. They were having a quiet ceremony at Mrs. Armbruster's house and there just wasn't a reason for anyone to travel. Within a couple of weeks her mother was bragging to her schoolteacher friends about how practical Ginny and her intended were being, by saving money for a house instead of a big wedding. She had them all believing it had been her idea, and that she advised Ginny so wisely. Another week or so and she believed it herself.

Greta was slow to forgive. When she and Chet made their announcement later that summer about being pregnant with Alton, Greta made a point of saying how many months they had been married. Mrs. Smith was all innocence and just replied, 'yes, or course dear," as if she didn't quite understand what Greta was getting at.

# 13

The Armbruster's

In the Spring of 1950, Ginny was making her first trip back home since she had left nearly six years before. It didn't seem possible that it had been so long. Her baby brother was a grown, married man and a father. She had been working at her law firm for almost four years and She and Danny had been married for over a year.

To save money that first year, Danny had moved in with her into her little apartment. Her single bed was replaced with a double which left even less room in the bedroom. They had to put a chest of drawers in the bathroom for Danny to have space for his clothes. But they were looking at houses now and it wouldn't be too long before they found the right place.

Ginny had never taken a vacation, so her wonderful boss had given her two weeks paid and a small bonus as a gift to pay for the trip. Danny had picked a time when they wouldn't be too busy at his shop and had left it all with his partner. Half of the time would be just making the drive there and back. That was ok. She and Danny would enjoy the trip together and it meant they only had to spend one week with Mother and JT. She had tried to stay in the little Starkville hotel, but Mother wouldn't hear of it, of course. Chet and Greta didn't have room for them, so Chet's old room was to be their vacation spot. His old room was in the attic, as far as he could possibly get from Mother and JT's room and that suited Ginny. The spare bedroom downstairs had been turned into JT's 'study', though no one knew what it was he was studying there.

She and Danny were driving Mrs. Armbruster's big old Buick. It was very roomy, and the plan was to pull over in campgrounds to sleep. Hopefully they could get a shower. They had some food in an ice chest and a gallon of tea. It would be easy to buy more groceries as they traveled.

She was anxious to see Chet again and couldn't wait to spoil that adorable nephew of hers, but she had another reason for wanting to spend a while in Arkansas. Even though she had never laid eyes on that place, it was a farm and reminded her of childhood. She wanted to kind of see if she could sleep without traffic noises and feel comfortable being out of town. As they had been house hunting, Danny had been driving further and further out of town looking for properties. He wasn't suggesting they take up farming, but they could get more house for the money, and He liked the idea of a garden and maybe a few horses. She knew he was thinking of children and the benefits of a country life, and she wanted children, too. She had just gotten very comfortable being a city girl.

To be fair, Danny wasn't suggesting she quit her job and stay home to milk goats or anything. He had kept his promise to let her be independent. Even though they both knew how much money the other one had in checking or savings accounts (or in the cookie jar, old habits die hard) they made their decisions together and paid expenses together. Ginny had to argue with Danny when he assumed he would take care of all the bills and her money was just hers. That was ridiculous since sometimes Danny's work was slow, and she made more than he did. Some months he made a lot, so it all worked out, but her job was good. While Ginny wanted to be independent, she also wanted to keep up her part as a teammate. In fact, that gave her independence. She had a say in the finances. She didn't have to worry that Danny would come home one night and say he had bought a farm with her money.

There wasn't much that made Ginny feel sorry for her mother, but the memory of that night did. All the years Mother had worked, saving all her money and then JT stole it all. The law may not look at it that way, but the law was wrong.

After three days on the road, she and Danny pulled off of the blacktop onto the dirt road per Chet's map and instructions. The road was unmarked, but Chet said it was about two miles from the intersection of state highways and to look for a barn with a colorful hex mark painted on the end. The barn was hard to miss, so she was sure they were in the right place. Chet's place was about a half mile in on the right, Mothers was a quarter mile further on the left. She had the urge to stop and see Chet first, but she knew her mother would make a fuss if she did. So, they drove on past. There was a pick-up truck in the yard, but there weren't any lights on in the house that she could see. The sun had just gone down, maybe they hadn't turned any lights on yet.

As they pulled into Mother's driveway, Ginny saw why there had been no lights on in Chet's cabin. He came walking out the front door, carrying the cutest, chubbiest baby she had ever seen, followed by a slender, beautiful woman, Mother and JT.

Danny barely had the car stopped before she threw herself out the door and jumped on Chet. She hugged him while practically smothering that baby with kisses. And no timid flower was he! Alton met his aunt's enthusiasm with a spasm of giggles that left him with hiccups that made him giggle more. The whole family was laughing. Even JT. Chet had mentioned that JT had a soft spot for Alton and called him "Boy" or "Jim- boy" (which made Greta grit her teeth).

As soon as the giggles subsided Chet turned and pulled Greta up beside him, "Ginny this is my Greta". Greta beamed at Ginny and said how glad she was to meet her.

"Chet, you told me she was pretty! That doesn't do this lady justice! Greta, you are a real beauty!" Greta smiled and ducked her head and tried to hide behind Chet. She wasn't used to much attention, and no one had ever said she was beautiful though Chet told her she was pretty, often enough. The truth was, being a wife and mother had brought out something special in her. A few pounds had given her a curvy figure, even though Chet could still fit his hands all the way around her waist. She was happy in her life, and it showed.

Danny came to the rescue, "Ginny, I think you are embarrassing the poor girl."

"Embarrass, my foot! She should know how beautiful she is! Goodness, Chet, don't you tell her?"

"I do, I swear!"

"You better!" She grabbed Danny's hand, "Family, this is my husband, Danny Armbruster." JT chose that point to remind everyone that he was the head of the family and stepped forward to shake Danny's hand.

"Mr. Armbruster, I'm JT Smith. Welcome."

"Nice to meet you Mr. Smith and Mrs. Smith," he said with a nod toward Ginny's mother. "Please, all of you, call me Danny."

Chet handed Alton to Ginny, since he was trying to climb out of his arms to get to her anyway and shook Danny's hand. "I sure am glad to meet you, Danny." I hope we can get to know each other this week."

"I hope so, too."

"So, Chet, how did you happen to be here? I had no idea when we would arrive."

"Aw Ginny, I could feel when you were getting close."

Greta chimed in, "It's true. I was trying to get dinner dishes done and he grabbed up Alton and said, 'Ginny will be here any minute. Let's go.' We hadn't been here five minutes before you pulled in."

Danny looked from Ginny to Chet, but neither of them found this to be as surprising as he and Greta did. Ginny explained, "He could always do that. As a baby, he knew when I was coming home from school. If I wandered off to be by myself, he always knew where I was. Playing hide and seek was never much fun."

"That's amazing." Danny had never heard of such a thing. Chet didn't really know what the big deal was. He shrugged.

Mother interrupted, "Have you had anything to eat? We have a ham in the refrigerator."

"Thank you, Mother, we are fine. We do have some food in the ice chest that I'd like to get in your refrigerator if there is room."

"We will make room. Let's get you settled in."

The next half hour was spent unloading the car, touring the house and finally getting their things carried up to the attic room. The windows were open, and it was cool and aired out but Ginny was glad they had not waited until later in the summer to come. It would be sweltering here in the hot months. And still better than having the room next to Mother and JT, so Ginny could see why Chet chose it.

Chet asked Danny, "Do you know how to ride a horse?"

He couldn't imagine anyone not knowing how, but he didn't know much about city people.

"I can manage not to fall off I think."

"Well, I don't think Old Buster will give you too much of a wild ride." Buster was the old plow horse Greta had learned to ride on, and her Daddy had let her bring him to their farm so that she and Chet could ride together. Sometimes she even helped him bring the cows in, but she had to get his mother to watch Alton, and she didn't like to leave him for long.

"I was thinking maybe in the morning we could take a ride, and I could show you the farms. The view is real nice from the ridge south of our place."

"It's a good thing it's got a nice view, it ain't good for much else," JT put in. JT never failed to point out the flaws with Chet's forty acres. It was true that the rocky ridge didn't have much for the cows to graze on, but there was good timber and Chet hoped someday he and Greta could build a house up there with a view of the valley.

"That sounds fine. What time do you want to head out?" Danny was excited to go for a ride and stretch his legs after three days in the car.

"I can have the horses saddled and over here by seven o'clock if that's ok."

"Sure, sounds fine."

Ginny said, "Oh no it doesn't. I'm not getting up at six to make breakfast. You better make that eight o'clock, Brother.

"I can make my own breakfast Ginny. We still have sandwich fixings."

"*I* will be making breakfast for everyone in the morning". Mother said, very firmly. "Chet, we will eat at seven-thirty, Greta if you and Alton would like to come, there will be plenty. You boys can ride after, and we can have a visit with Alton. Does that sound good?"

Actually, it did. They all nodded in agreement. Gretta grabbed Alton up off of the floor and she and Chet said their goodbyes. It was past the baby's bedtime, and he was asleep on Greta's shoulder before they made it out of the yard.

As they walked home in the moonlight, Greta said, "I really like your sister."

"Just because she said you are beautiful!"

"Chet, stop! That was silly!"

Chet pulled her close and looked at her in the moonlight, with their son sleeping like an angel on her shoulder. She was beautiful. That lovely girl he had met in Grove had blossomed into a beautiful woman, right under his nose. "Greta, it's not silly. I'm just sorry Ginny had to tell you that before I did. You are beautiful. And Alton is beautiful. And I am a lucky saddle-tramp. (Bill had told him of Earl's first impression of him and it was a running joke.)

Greta leaned her head on Chet's chest for a minute. If this was the influence Ginny had on Chet, she could stay! Chet didn't usually share how he felt. She knew, she really did, but gosh it was nice to hear.

After a minute she pulled away and they continued their walk home.

# 14

◈

# The Visit

Chet was surprised but Danny actually rode quite well. They spent the morning going around JT and Mother's farm, showing him the corral, the big old barn, the spring-fed stream that ran through with cool, clear water. He showed him the fences he had worked so hard to build on his place, the lean-to's he had built as cattle sheds and finally, they ended up on top of the ridge behind the cabin, looking at the whole valley. It *was* a beautiful sight. They made their way down to the cabin and tied the horses out front. Chet loosened the girth straps on both horses and said he would let them cool a while before he took them to unsaddle.

They went into the cabin and found Ginny and Greta working together in the kitchen to get lunch ready. "Your mother is insisting that she is doing dinner tonight, but I convinced her that we could manage lunch." Greta smiled as Chet dropped a kiss on her forehead.

"Good girl. Where is Alton?" Chet asked as he walked to the sink to wash his hands. He motioned for Danny to join him, and they both lathered up under the cold running water. They didn't have a water heater yet, but Greta was so proud of having water right in the house. No more carrying buckets!

"The last I saw he was on his floor, telling his life story to that monkey Ginny gave him." This morning at breakfast Ginny had given him a sock monkey that a girlfriend of hers made. The eyes were felt instead of buttons and wouldn't pull off. Alton had squealed and started chattering to his new friend and hadn't stopped. He had shown his monkey every toy in his room.

When Chet went to look in on him, that was exactly what he was doing. Sitting in a pile of toys and babbling non-stop. Occasionally, he would shake the monkey, like he was making sure he was paying attention.

Ginny walked up and peaked around Chet to watch him. The movement caught his eye and Alton beamed up at her and yelled, "GINNEEE" at the top of his lungs. Chet was stunned. Greta and Danny came running. Greta said, "Did Alton just say Ginny?"

"He did." Alton babbled all the time. Occasionally you could make out a 'mama' or a 'dadada' but nothing so clear.

Ginny stepped over the half-door and knelt by him. "What did you say, honey?"

"Ginneee."

Ginny was near tears, and she grabbed that little boy and snuggled him until he squealed. "Oh, I have got to get me one of these!

Danny shook his head, "Thanks a lot kid." But he was pretty pleased to hear it. The sooner the better, as far as he was concerned.

Greta huffed in an act of dismay, "Well I guess I know who rates around here. Not the woman who feeds him or bathes him but the one who gives him a stuffed monkey! Well!" But she was so proud. He had said Ginny's name very clearly. More words would follow soon. Her little guy was growing up so fast.

Ginny grabbed Alton and his monkey and took him to the kitchen to sit in his highchair. Monkey sat on the windowsill and Alton started to fuss until Greta sat a bowl of green peas in front of him and that caught his attention. She wasn't sure if he liked peas, but she knew he liked chasing them around the bowl with his pudgy little fingers and trying to get them in his mouth. Very few ended up on the floor so overall it was a success. It kept him busy anyway.

They sat down to a dinner of cube-steak, potatoes, gravy and green peas. Greta gave Alton bites of potatoes and gravy in between his bites of peas.

Danny looked at the spread in front of him and said, "It's a good thing we are only here for a week. I would gain a ton eating like this every day."

"Aw, we would work it off of ya", Chet chuckled.

The days flew by. Chet and Ginny caught up on all the little things they had been missing and Danny and Greta enjoyed seeing them together. Ginny even spent some time with her mother, going through photo albums and scrapbooks. It was a wonderful week and Ginny wished they had more time to spend.

She had time to think over Danny's desire to live out of town and realized country life isn't so bad when you aren't being worked to death. She and Danny both had good jobs, so it wouldn't be like that. She had actually enjoyed the peace and quiet this week and she remembered how much fun she had had gardening with Mrs. Armbruster. Maybe she would enjoy a small garden. She would talk it over with Danny on the drive home.

The afternoon before they were to leave, Ginny and Greta were helping Mother in the kitchen. She wanted to put on a big feast and send them with leftovers to eat on the road. She had two chickens to cut up to fry, figuring there would be a few pieces they could take to eat cold. She was making a huge amount of potato salad. They were getting potatoes and eggs to boil when they heard a crash from the front room. They all ran to see what was happening and found JT on the living room floor. It looked like he had tried to stand up from his chair and had collapsed forward onto the rug. Greta rolled him gently onto his back. He was breathing, and his eyes were open, but he looked all wrong. His face was all pulled down on the left side.

"Oh, my Lord", Mother gasped, covering her mouth with both hands. "He's having a stroke!"

Ginny grabbed the telephone and dialed "o" to get the operator. She asked to be connected to the local ambulance service. She was surprised to hear the phone answered as "Funeral Home" but she asked if they could connect her with an ambulance service and found she had the right number after all. She gave her details, and they said they would send a car as soon as possible.

Mother was pressing a cool cloth to JT's face and Greta had a pillow under his head. Mother suggested calling Doctor Jeffries while they waited for the ambulance. Ginny got him and the phone and filled him in on the details. He said he would meet the ambulance at the hospital in Grove.

After what seemed like days, they heard a siren and soon the ambulance turned into the driveway. The attendants were getting JT onto a stretcher when Chet's truck pulled up and he and Danny ran to the house, Alton clinging to Chet as he ran.

They burst through the door and saw JT loaded on the stretcher. Chet and Danny both breathed a sigh of relief to see that their wives were ok. Then they took in what was going on. "What happened here?" Chet asked Greta as she moved to take Alton in her arms.

Your mother thinks he had a stroke. Doctor Jeffries said he could meet them at the hospital.

They got JT loaded into the ambulance/hearse and got the stretcher strapped down. They led mother to a passenger door and said she could ride with them. Ginny ran from the house and handed Mother her purse." We will stay here, Mother. Call us when you know something."

They stood in the yard and watched the ambulance make its way back out to the blacktop. Ginny leaned on Danny and Chet and Greta held their son between them. For a while no one spoke, then it seemed like a dam burst and they all talked at once.

"When we heard the sirens, I just didn't know what to think." "I was so relieved to see you." "We just heard a crash." "He looked so small and weak."

After a few minutes the shock started to wear off and Ginny said, "I guess the best plan is to continue as we were. We have chicken to fry and potato salad to make."

Chet nodded, "We can't do nothin' till she calls. If I can leave Alton here, I'll go get the cows fed so that's done if we need to go somewhere."

"Of course, he's showing his blocks to his monkey. He would scream if you tried to move him, anyway." Alton had made his way to the toy locker that Grandmother kept for him near the old fireplace in the kitchen. The fireplace had been sealed and was no longer usable, so it made a cubby that Alton had claimed as his own play spot. Grandmother had pulled a braided rag rug in for him, so it was comfy if he happened to fall asleep there. Which he did often.

Danny stood, "I'll go with you. Maybe I can help."

Chet nodded, "We'll make a hand of you yet."

After the men left, Ginny and Greta settled into dinner preparations, but both were still shaken. Ginny broke the silence, "You know JT was never my favorite person but seeing him drop like that, when he looked like his normal self an hour before, well it was a shock."

"He is a hard man to love, that's true enough, but he looked scared. My heart went out to him."

"I guess no one deserves that. Not even JT."

Chet and Danny returned, dinner was served, and Alton was put to bed on couch cushions shoved in his fireplace cubby. Still no call from Mother. Chet and Greta didn't want to go back to their house, in case she called, and it was Ginny and Danny's last night here. At least that was the plan.

"I suppose I could call the office in the morning and explain the situation. I might be able to extend my vacation by a day or two."

"We just don't know what to do until we hear from your mother. We should just pack our things and wait. No harm in that."

Around eight-thirty the phone rang. Ginny answered and spoke with her mother. Chet, Danny and Greta were straining to hear, but they didn't interrupt as Ginny made notes and talked to her mother in hushed tones. "Yes, Mother, I can do that. Of course, if you think it's best. Should Danny and I stay another day? No, that's not a problem, we will see you then."

She hung up the phone and turned to give her report. "It was indeed a stroke. He is resting now, and there is no way to know how much damage was done. Right now, he can't talk or move his left arm. Mother is staying with him tonight. I offered to bring her night clothes, but she said she was fine for tonight. It is likely to be a good while JT can leave the hospital. She gave me a list of things to bring her tomorrow morning."

"Will we be staying another day or two then?" Danny asked as he came to put his arms around Ginny. "We can if we need to."

"No, Mother says there is no need. We can't know how long it will be before his condition changes. I did tell her we would bring things to her in the morning and say our goodbyes then. It will delay our start by a few hours, but we can make that up on the trip."

"Sure, we can. That's no problem."

Greta asked, "How can we help? What should we be doing?"

"Oh, you have the hard part, honey," Ginny said in her matter-of-fact way. "We will see Mother in the morning and then head back to California. You have to stay here and pick up the pieces."

Chet said, "I know I'll be taking care of the cattle for JT."

"You will have to get Mother back and forth to the hospital and when JT comes home, he will need care". Ginny continued thoughtfully, "No matter how much he recovers, I don't think he will be the same."

"That could be a blessing," Chet muttered.

"Or not." Ginny raised an eyebrow. "JT has never been one to look on the bright side."

Greta took the list from Ginny, "Well let's at least get these things packed up. I'll help you get food put away and packed for your trip. It doesn't look like Mother will be coming home to eat any chicken tonight. But then we need to get Alton in his own bed. If we wait too long to move him, he will be up the rest of the night."

They tidied up and said goodnight. Chet and Greta promised to be back in the morning for a quick breakfast before Danny and Ginny left. Chet was getting glum at the idea that Ginny was leaving. He had missed her every day, and it had been so good to have her here.

# 15

## Back to Bakersfield

Ginny and Danny got a late start, it was nearly noon before they got on the road west. Chet and Greta had breakfast with them and then said they would do the cleaning so Ginny and Danny could get going. They carried the last of their things and the cooler of food to the car and hugged everyone, one more time. Ginny handed Alton back to Greta and said, "Goodbye sweet boy." Alton inhaled a big breath and shouted "'bye Ginneee!" and grabbed his monkey and squeezed him tight.

Everyone laughed and Alton smiled and looked proud of himself. He waved until their car was out of sight. Chet and Greta went in to straighten up the house and close it up, before heading back to their routine. It was going to be strange to not have Ginny and Danny here. They had gotten so used to them being here.

Ginny and Danny drove to the hospital and found Mother dozing at JT's bedside. JT looked awful, but he was alive, that was something. Mother hugged Ginny and cried. She wanted to ask Ginny to stay but she knew they had to get back. She told Danny how wonderful it had been to meet him and to take care of her sweet Ginny. They settled her back in with JT and made their escape as soon as they could.

When they were finally on the road, Ginny said, "It was so good to see Chet and Greta and the baby and I'm glad we came. But I'm so very glad we don't have to stay. I'm sorry for what Mother and JT are going through, but I don't think I could stand to be here much longer. I feel a little like I am abandoning Chet all over again, though."

"I know that you miss Chet, and he would rather see you more often, too, but I don't think Chet could leave any more than you could stay. He might like to visit us in Bakersfield someday, but I don't think he would ever want to live there. He has an attachment to his land and his cows that goes deep. I saw that this week."

"That's true. Speaking of living in Bakersfield, would you mind if we didn't?"

"Danny was caught off guard, "What do you mean?"

"There was a nice little home in Shafter that we looked at. It was a Spanish style with a few grape vines, a small pool out back, about ten acres if I remember correctly. It might be nice to live there."

Danny had to be careful to turn his attention back to the road. He was so surprised by what Ginny was saying he had almost driven off the road. "Do you mean that?"

"It would be pretty mean of me to say if I didn't. So, yes, I mean it. If that place is still available, I would like to make an offer on it. If it's not, we can look for another. It will mean driving in to work every day, which means we need a car, too. That will be another expense. But just think how much we will save on grapes?!"

"Yes, I'm sure the savings on grapes will offset the other expenses."

They both managed to hold a straight face for about ten seconds before they burst out laughing. The next three days on the road were spent laughing and chatting about how they imagined their life would be in their new home.

They made it home late on Saturday night. They spent Sunday unloading the car and settling back into being home. Sunday night they had dinner with Mom to tell her their plans for buying a home. On Monday morning, on her break at work, Ginny called the realtor to say that she and her husband might be interested in the Ranchette in Shafter. By Monday night, contacts were signed, and Danny and Ginny were well on their way to being homeowners.

# 16

## Mother's Choices

A week after Ginny and Danny left for California, JT was released from the hospital. Mother had arranged for a hospital bed to put in JT's study and had a local woman hired to help her around the house. Mrs. Fleming wasn't a nurse by training, but she had a good deal of experience with taking care of invalids. Doctor Jeffries had recommended her and since part of her pay was in room and board, the expense was not too bad. She was moving into Chet's old attic room and claimed it suited her just fine. It was weeks before school started so Mother would have time to get JT into a routine before she left him with Mrs. Fleming during the days.

JT had not recovered any use of his left side. He could stand for a few seconds but couldn't really walk. They moved his recliner near the hospital bed so he could, with help, move from one place to another. Doctor Jeffries said the best way to prevent bedsores was to make sure he moved often and to change his sheets daily. The laundry alone justified having Mrs. Fleming to help.

JT *had* recovered a great deal of his speech. His words were slurred, but he made himself understood. The second day he was home, he wanted to know how Chet had been taking care of his cattle. Chet tried to reassure him that he had done everything just as JT would have done but, as usual, JT didn't think he could have possibly done anything right. It came as a shock to both JT and Chet when Mother settled that argument.

"I sold your cattle to Mr. Selfridge, and I leased him the pasture that adjoins his property, the eighty acres on the west. Chet, you can use the barn and pasture on the east side for your cattle in return for keeping the property taken care of, fences, mowing and the like. Do we have a deal?"

"Well sure, that's easy enough!"

"JT looked like he was going to have another stroke, right then and there. "Woman, have you lost your mind? His words may have been slurred but his meaning was clear enough. "You have no right to make deals on my property without my say so."

"Oh, don't I? Like when you bought this farm with my money without asking me? Maybe it was legal, but it wasn't right. Well, this is legal and right. Doctor Jeffries wrote a statement that you are currently unfit to handle business affairs. The judge took his advice and gave me power of attorney. I had my contracts with Mr. Selfridge signed and notarized at the bank yesterday." She turned to Chet, "I don't think we need a contract do we Chet?"

"No ma'am, I'm clear on the terms."

"Well then, we are settled."

JT was anything but settled. "How dare you bamboozle a doctor and a judge to allow you to steal my money. You just wait until I'm better."

"We will cross that bridge *if we* come to it. As for, how I dare; how do you think I paid for a hospital bed to be delivered, or hired Mrs. Fleming, or paid for the other expenses? You would be hard put to prove I stole anything since it has all been spent on you."

Chet had occasionally felt that his mother might be proud of what he had done with his life so far, but he had never been this proud of her! He didn't know when she had even found the time to accomplish all of this. It turned out Doctor Jeffries had played a large role. He had seen this done before and knew how to present everything to the judge. He had given mother a ride to meet with the judge and Mr. Selfridge had taken her to the bank. Chet was in awe. He could see a little of Ginny in their mother and had never seen that before. There may not be a lot of love in their relationship, but there was a growing respect.

JT had no answer for how the expenses had been met because it hadn't occurred to him to care. He was still fuming but he knew he had been beat. Bested by that woman and her cur offspring. He turned his face to the wall and asked to be left alone.

As they left the room, Mother gave Chet more instructions. "I want you to drive all of JT's stock over to the western pasture as soon as you can. Mr. Selfridge will take over from there. You can start moving your cattle onto the eastern fields anytime you like. And Chet, you have been buying calves to feed up and sell for years now, don't you think it's time to keep a more permanent herd?"

"Well ma'am my place doesn't have good winter pasture. That's why I've always sold most all of them off."

"I understand but there is two hundred acres of good pasture on the east side, and the creek besides. That should solve your problems there. If you consider getting a more permanent herd, don't take a loan from the bank this time. At least not until we have talked. I may have some money to invest."

"Well ma'am, I have been talking to the ranchers hereabouts about the Angus cattle. Folks are starting to care more about where their beef comes from, and the Angus is getting very popular. I had hoped to buy more Angus cows in the future."

"It sounds like you have been thinking on it. Well, I'll tell you what I was thinking then. I own a good piece of land. I could lease it all to Selfridge, he wanted it, but I held back the best until I could talk to you. I want you to look around for good breeding stock. I know I can trust your judgment there; you know what you are looking for. Find what you want and let me know how much per head. Find us a good bull, one with sound bloodlines. The bull is where we don't scrimp. I'll see how many head we can afford. I will pay the upfront cost, and you will do *all* the work. Greta and I will keep a ledger of expenses, I know you don't have a head for that, but I think she might. I'm willing to split the profit fifty-fifty. How does that sound?"

To Chet, it sounded like Christmas came early. It sounded like all of his Christmases came at once. He would say his dreams came true, but he had never dreamed this big. At least not that his mother would be his Santy Claus!

He grabbed his mother up and hugged her! Actually, *hugged her.* Lifted her right off the floor. He had never really noticed how tiny she was, she had always loomed so large in his life.

"Chester, you put me down right now!" She did her best to sound put out, but she was smiling. "I take it you find those terms agreeable?"

"Yes ma'am, I agree to those terms."

"Ok, then go on home and talk it over with Greta. See if she has any thoughts."

"Yes *ma'am*! He ran for the door, "Thank you", he called over his shoulder as he ran down the driveway.

Greta had put Alton down for a nap and was getting pork chops out to thaw for dinner, when she saw Chet legging it up the hill like he was on fire. She threw the pork chops on the counter and ran out the back door to meet him. He never slowed down, but just scooped her in his arms and kept running until they were in the little garden behind the house. He let out a big "Whoopee", kissed her on the mouth and set her down.

Greta was dazed. Chet had gone to talk to JT about cows. What had happened over there?

Chet said, "Greta, you won't believe it. You won't believe it. You should have seen her! Oh, you should have seen *him*! And we are set! I mean, we can't go spending, but in a couple of years maybe... Greta do you know what this *means*?

"No Chet, I have no idea what this means. Do I need to call someone? Have you lost your mind?"

"No, I haven't…. well maybe…but no, I'm pretty sure it happened…we will have to check."

"Ok Chet, now you are starting to scare me. What in the world happened?"

"A miracle darlin'. Nothing short of a miracle. Let's go in the house and I'll tell ya."

"Not until you are under control, Alton is asleep."

"I'm fine now, I'll be … well, wait……Whooppeeeee! Now I'm fine."

Whoopee? Chet said whoopee? Greta wasn't sure he was fine at all.

In the end, Greta was the one that woke Alton from his nap. Chet explained the entire conversion to Greta, from Mother telling JT off, to the deal he made with her. Part of the time she had both hands over her mouth in disbelief but by the time he finished telling her everything, she opened her mouth to speak and shouted, "Whoopee!" She was red faced when she heard Alton start to cry and went to get him while Chet laughed.

That evening they did the unheard of and placed a long-distance call to Danny and Ginny. They held the phone between them so they could both hear.

"Ginny, it's Chet."

"Chet, what's wrong?"

"Nothing is wrong Ginny, I just wanted to tell you…"

"Well, you can't afford to make long distance calls if…"

"GINNY! Let me talk so I *don't* have to get a loan to pay Grove Telephone next month."

"Ok, Chet, I'm sorry"

Chet told her how their mother had taken control of JT's property and the deal she had made him.

"Chet, I am so happy for you. It was the right thing to do, but JT would never have done it."

"I am starting to think our mother may have the better head for business."

"That would make sense. She did manage to go to college and set herself up. Her biggest mistake was letting JT have any control."

"Ginny gets it from somewhere", apparently Danny was listening, too.

Ginny said, "Danny and I have some news of our own. I was just writing you a letter."

"Oh, what's going on? Greta asked. "Oh! Are you expecting?!"

"Ginny laughed, "No, not yet. But we bought a house!"

"A house! Where?"

"Well Chet, you won't believe it. We bought a farm, about a half hour from Bakersfield."

"You did not!"

Ginny laughed. Danny said, "Don't tease him, Ginny. We bought a little place with some grapevines and a little pasture. Only ten acres. We aren't going into farming or ranching just yet."

"Well, I'll be. Ginny on a farm." Chet was nearly speechless. What a day for surprises.

Ginny said, "Hey Chet, I think our three minutes are up! I'll write to you! Greta, write to me with all the details. And send me pictures of that sweet baby!

She hung up before Chet could argue. Those calls cost a fortune.

Chet sat by the phone table in silence for a minute. "Mother in the cattle business and Ginny on a farm. I want to hurry and go to bed so I can wake up tomorrow and see if it's all still real."

"It will be, Honey. It all really happened.

~~~

Ginny hung up the phone with Chet and went back to the sofa, where she had been curled up by Danny, reading a book. They had discussed buying a TV set but with the upcoming purchase of the house and the car they would have to have, TV was on the backburner. She wasn't sure she wanted to give up her quiet evenings anyway.

She curled back up by Danny, but she couldn't go back to her book, just yet. She sat and stared at nothing for a while as she imagined the
~~~

coup that Mother had pulled. All these many years, Ginny had always thought her mother gave away her choices when she married JT, but she had waited quietly for her chance.

And speaking of chance: Fat chance JT had of doing anything about it now. If he jumped up in a week healthy as a horse and reversed her power of attorney, he couldn't undo the deals she had made. She would be able to show that the money made had been for JT's health care and her plan of leasing the pasture and going in business with Chet was going to make more money than JT's little herd ever would. Mother's paycheck had been keeping them afloat.

Now, Mother was a teacher, which she loved, a landlord, a cattle rancher and had live-in help. My how things could change in a week. If Ginny had known that JT having a stroke would be such a force of good, she would have thrown him out of a barn loft long ago. Lord knows, Chet's life would have been easier.

But just look at Chet! Just about to turn twenty-one years old and he had a beautiful wife (and no bones about it, Greta was beautiful) a sweet, happy little boy, a house he built with his own hands and made improvements on daily, and let's not forget, he was managing it all by selling his calves and doing odd side-jobs. But now, with Mother backing him, he could really make something of himself. He had a knack with livestock. Ginny was sure this was his opportunity.

She noticed Danny wasn't reading his book either. He was watching her. "Have you worked through it now?"

She smiled up at him, "I think I made a good start. I just can't believe Mother did all that. I was picturing her falling apart with no one to make decisions. I thought Chet would have to step in. I guess I have really underestimated her. So, that part I haven't quite worked through yet."

"No. I imagine that will take some time."

"Well, I don't think I'm going to figure it all out tonight. Let's go to bed."

"Oh! Mrs. Armbruster! I like how you think!"

"Oh! Mr. Armbruster! You can read my mind!" Ginny giggled and led him to the bedroom.

<h1 style="text-align:center">17</h1>

<h1 style="text-align:center">El Rancho</h1>

It had been a whirlwind, moving from their small Bakersfield apartment to the *Rancho de Armbruster* in Shafter. First there had been loan paperwork, inspections, real estate contracts and a thousand small decisions to make. Fortunately, the law firm that Ginny worked for had a division that handled real estate law, so she was able to get some guidance. But she had to be careful to work on it during her free time. She had built a good reputation for herself, and she didn't want to be seen as taking advantage.

Danny's military service helped them secure a good loan, and, ultimately with a long mortgage and a good rate, they were paying very little more for the mortgage than the rent on her apartment. With the way prices were booming in the years since the war, rents in town were increasing. They had made a good decision to move out of town when they did. It wouldn't be long before the city moved out to them!

The drive to work wasn't bad at all. They rode together, with Ginny dropping Danny at the airfield before she went onto the office. Usually by the time she was back to pick him up he was just wiping his hands and putting away tools. One expense with the move that couldn't be avoided was a new car. Mom Armbruster had tried to give them the Buick, and though they loved it for traveling, it was a *lot* of car for the daily commute. They talked Mom into keeping it for herself and they bought a *brand-new 1951 Ford Custom* two-door sedan. It was powder blue and Ginny thought it was the prettiest thing she had ever seen. It was fun to drive it into the city every day and park in her space at the office.

The property was more amazing than Ginny had remembered. The first time they had seen it, she had been skeptical of moving out of town, so maybe she didn't give it her full attention. She did remember that of the places they looked at she felt the most drawn to this one. The house was set back from the road with a long gravel drive. Grapevines lined the drive about halfway to the house. There was a large tree in the yard that Ginny learned was called a 'Coast Live Oak' and it provided shade to the front of the house. The house was a Spanish adobe style and was a pale beige, almost pink color. It was more of a bungalow than a hacienda, just one-story with an archway into an alcove to the front door. The wood was stained dark, and the hardware was heavy, like wrought iron. Inside the floors were hard wood, with red clay tile in the kitchen and bathroom. It had two bedrooms and a full dining room, with a little foyer by the front door leading to the living room. A massive window in the living room looked out at the shade tree and you could see the grapevines from there.

In the back, there was the little swimming pool. Not Olympic size by any means, but big enough to swim a few strokes. Definitely big enough to float in on hot summer days! A few more trees were in the back yard, but not as massive as the one in front. There was a small, detached garage, and there was a small apartment on the backside of that garage. It was just a little studio unit with a three-quarter bath, and it had obviously just been used for storage for quite some time. The whole property was fenced and there were a couple of sheds intended for livestock shelter. Danny hoped to have horses someday, he had really enjoyed riding with Chet.

The next item to tackle was furniture. Ginny had bought well when she furnished her apartment. She had known what she wanted and had bought good furniture. But this house seemed enormous compared to the apartment. When the living room furniture was all in the room still looked empty. Ginny was, of course, scared to spend when they had just taken on so much more, but Danny again, talked her into having a look.

"Ginny, we did well on the mortgage and the car. We aren't spending much more than we were in the apartment. And remember, we are saving a fortune on grapes!"

"I'm not sure how much you think we were spending on grapes before!" The truth was, there was about an acre in grapevines, and they had more grapes than they knew what to do with. They had plenty to eat and share and Mom had helped Ginny bottle grape juice and make grape jelly. Next year they would be more prepared. A neighbor had promised to show them how to tend the vines and they would probably add a few more plants. They hadn't even tried to sell any this year since they were so busy with the move.

"Well, I know we aren't spending it now. Let's go see Ted."

They drove to Ted's store. Ted had expanded to add more showroom area and now sold some new furniture as well as the used. He had another location in town, but he could usually be found here, he still kept his hand in on the refinishing.

"He saw them come in and, like always, greeted them enthusiastically. "Well, if it isn't the beautiful Ginny! How come you never come see me without this guy?" He punched Danny in the shoulder.

"Because I'm Little Red Riding Hood and you're the Big Bad Wolf! Hello, Ted how have you been?" She took Ted's hands and kissed him on the cheek.

"Hey now, where's mine?" Danny tried to play the jealous husband, but he grinned too much.

"Don't worry Sport, plenty for you!" Before Danny could move, he had planted a kiss on his cheek.

"Not at all what I meant."

"Well now that you have scared off half of your customers, why don't you show us some furniture?"

"My customers'? Are you kidding? They come here for the show!"

Ginny looked around and noticed a new section of the showroom. "Ted, are those televisions?"

"Yes, ma'am and you are looking at a freshly minted technician of the radio and television industry. In other words, I took night classes in TV repair."

"I knew you were smart. Didn't I say he was smart?"

"You did. And what's more, after all these years you haven't changed your mind."

"It's such a natural fit. He could already repair the cabinets, now he can work on the sets."

"Not much different than us taking apart Mom's old radio, is it?"

"Don't you believe that for a minute Danny-Boy. And don't you ever take the back off your set! Those things store enough energy to kill you, even unplugged."

"Yikes. I won't! Thanks for the heads up, even though we don't own a set."

"Yet, Danny boy, yet."

"I can't believe I fell into that one. I"

Ginny took his hand, "I can't either, dear."

It was from that point inevitable. He knew Ginny's weakness for sleek modern design and led them to the set she couldn't resist. It was a *Zenith Black Magic* similar in wood grain to their living room furniture. The stunning part was that it was the *newest* model, but since it had been a demonstration model at Ted's school, he got it very cheaply and of course was passing his savings on. Ginny wondered how he ever made money if he treated everyone the way he treated them. He promised to help set this up with a big enough antenna so that they would be able to watch it clearly.

They needed a couple of extra chairs for the living room and now with the TV set, Ginny was rethinking how to arrange. Now she was thinking of their existing furniture would be in a grouping with sofa in the middle of the room. That sofa table would actually go behind the sofa now. Then the TV against the wall on the opposite side of the room with two chairs facing it. Maybe an end table between the chairs.

She started running her ideas by Ted. He had a running inventory in his head and if she described what she wanted, he would know where to find it.

The kitchen table she had from the apartment now had a kitchen that it fit in just fine. They had no dining room furniture at all. They had the mix-matched bed, nightstand and chest of drawers from the apartment and Ginny thought they worked fine for the spare bedroom, but she wanted a nice set for their bedroom.

She started to crumble at the amounts that were adding up in her head. The television was a good deal. The chairs were affordable. But they didn't *need* a dining table or a bedroom set.

Danny could see the gears turning and took Ginny aside. "Honey, we have been here before. You know Ted will take payments and work with us. Just look for the things you like. This is our home! We are allowed to have it the way we want it."

"But we don't need it all at once, Danny. I can wait."

"But why wait when we don't have to Ginny? You make good money. I make good money and if we got in a bind, I could give myself a raise. Mark and I agreed to leave money in the business for future expansion, but the money is there. Don't fret."

"Why Danny, are we rich?" she teased.

"Nope. But well-enough off that we can have furniture for the house we both work for."

"Ok, you win. You always win."

"Aw, it's sweet of you to let me think so."

Ted reappeared from the warehouse. He had wandered off while Ginny was looking at the dining tables.

"Hey kids, come look out back. I've got something you will want to see."

He showed them to a spot where he had set up a dining table with six matching chairs. It was a medium tan wood with beautiful grain. The chairs had slightly curved backs with plain vertical slats, and beige upholstered seats. The table and chairs were both a bit scuffed, you could tell Ted hadn't worked his magic here yet.

"Beautiful! What is this wood, Ted?"

"Thank you for asking. It's teak. Lightweight but very strong."

"Teak. Hmmm. It's a nice set."

"A set like this will last a lifetime. This is real craftmanship."

"I notice a few scratches."

"Yeah, I just got it in. But I thought of you because it's your style and the scratches are light. It won't need to be totally redone."

"I do like it."

"I just got this load of furniture from a family that moved here from Hawaii. They had all their furniture shipped here and then the wife decided she wanted Early American. No accounting for taste, huh?"

"I guess not"

"So now look at this!" He pulled dust covers from two nearby pieces. There was a tall china hutch and a low buffet. Both in the same teak, with nickel hardware.

"Oh Ted, they are perfect." They really were, there wasn't a scratch that she could see. "Danny, what do you think."

"I like whatever you like. You know that."

"This is for our house. I want you to like it, too."

"Ginny, you have better taste than I do. I trust your judgment and I will love it."

"Listen to the man, he is obviously intelligent."

In the end, as Danny had predicted, Ted worked with them on a good deal and they got the dining room set, the TV, chairs and end table for the living room and a blond wood bedroom set with two nightstands, a dresser, a chest of drawers and a queen-size bed. This was where Danny finally had an opinion. Ginny had argued against the bed.

"We will have to get new sheets and it's just ridiculously large."

"We will still use the sheets on the bed in the spare bedroom and you have seen how tiny our bed looks in that big room. This will fit better in the room. I like this set.

Since Ginny had picked everything else, she couldn't argue.

When it came to the mattress and springs, he was picky, too. He picked out a 'pocket spring' box spring and a medium firm mattress with matching beige fabric.

"What does it matter what they look like when they will be covered up?"

"I'll know. I like them."

Again, how could she argue.

Since they had gone furniture shopping on Saturday and had to work all week, they arranged for it all to be delivered the following Saturday. Ted said that would give him time to get the antenna and wire he would need to install their television.

Ginny could hardly wait to see it all in the house. She took magazines to work to show the other secretaries the style her furniture was, though it was never an exact match. The girls all envied her. Most of the girls she worked with were single and lived in apartments. Many of the girls that she had graduated from Bakersfield College with quit working when they got married, so there were new girls in all the time. She couldn't imagine working that hard to get through college just to walk away when she got married. Of course, some girls started with that goal in mind; to work in an office and meet a man to marry. That had never been Ginny's goal. She was lucky with Danny, who understood how she felt.

Even though she didn't see marriage as the salvation of a woman, she did have a happy marriage herself and wanted that for her friends. In fact, Natalie, who had just started in her office, was a sweet girl with a sense of humor. She seemed perfect for Ted.

She brought it up with Danny that night. "Danny, since Ted is going to be here on Saturday anyway, why don't we ask him to stay for dinner? We can christen the dining table."

"That sounds fine."

"And that new girl at my office, Natalie? I was thinking of inviting her. I think she and Ted would hit it off."

"If you want to invite her, that's fine. But don't go expecting to make a match there. Natalie isn't Ted's type."

"How can you say that? You haven't even really met the girl."

"Honey, Ted is a confirmed bachelor."

"Oh." She scoffed and waved her hand at Danny. "That's because he hasn't met the right girl."

"Darling, I'm trying to tell you, there isn't a 'right girl' for Ted."

"How can you say that? Ted is tall and handsome and funny..."

"He is all those things. But Ted isn't interested in the girls in your office. He might like to meet some of the attorneys though."

"Why would Ted need an attorney?"

"Ginny, my love, you are the smartest woman, no, the smartest person that I know, but you aren't making this easy."

Ginny scrunched her face, "Making what easy?"

"Ginny, Ted doesn't like women."

Ginny still looked confused. Then realization hit.

"There ya go."

"Danny, you must be joking. Ted's not a, not a ...."

"A man who prefers the company of men."

"No! I mean he's over six feet tall!"

"Six four. But I didn't realize there was a height requirement."

"You're not funny! I mean he isn't at all effete."

"Honey you are so worldly that sometimes I forget you are just a little ol' farm girl, aren't you?"

"Why are you picking on me?"

"I'm not. I think it's adorable that you think that homosexual men are all short and effeminate."

"I don't.... well, I guess I did."

"Darlin' I've known Ted since first grade and since we knew the difference in boys and girls Ted has known which he prefers. He doesn't carry a sign, but he doesn't hide it either. It's not as unusual as you think either. I was in the Army with hundreds of men. There are some that don't like women. It's not that big of a deal."

"There are homosexual men in the Army?"

Danny couldn't help himself at that one, he laughed out loud. "Oh, honey yes. Wherever there are men, there are homosexuals."

"I do feel a little naive, I guess."

"Nothing wrong with that. But maybe don't get Natalie's hopes up."

"Oh right, I'm glad I hadn't mentioned it to her."

Ted came in his car on Saturday, the delivery truck following him with all of the furniture and two men to carry it all. The men carried the furniture in and laid out the antennae and poles for the television then returned the truck to the store. Ted stayed to help move furniture in place and to set up the television. He worked with Danny to put the bed frame together and get the mattress on. Ginny watched them work together, laughing and joking like brothers. She had seen them together many times and she just couldn't see anything about Ted that was *different* from any other friend of Danny's or Chet's.

She didn't feel any different about Ted. She realized that it really wasn't any of her business, but she was just confused. Everything that she had heard whispered about homosexuals, and granted it wasn't much, was that they were weak men, effeminate, not big strong men.

Since it really was none of her business she gave up on her pondering and started on the mountain of work still to be done. After the boys were done getting the bedroom furniture in place they went to work on the television. She had shown Danny exactly where she wanted it so that he and Ted could decide how to run the wire and place the antenna. She stayed in the bedroom to put the new bedding on the bed. She had purchased sheets, mattress pads, blankets and a spread earlier this week and washed all of it and aired it on the line. It was all fresh and ready to make up the bed.

Next, she used rolls of paper and lined the drawers in the dresser and chest of drawers and put some sachets of cedar wood in each drawer in preparation of putting clothes away.

As she toiled away in the bedroom Danny and Ted worked outside to put the pole up for the antenna. Ted said, "Ginny sure seems quiet today. Is she ok?"

"She's fine, she is just studying you a bit."

"Studying me? Why?"

"Well, she wanted to set you up with one of the girls from her office and I suggested that she not."

"She wanted to set.... we have known each other for years... did she not know?"

"She did not. I don't think she knew it was possible. You're too tall for one thing."

"Too tall... Oh my goodness." He laughed and shook his head. "I see, I'm supposed to be five-foot-five, limp wristed and talk with a lisp?"

"That's pretty much the picture. Don't hold it against her. She just had a very sheltered upbringing."

"Oh, I would never hold it against her. Ginny is a doll. Should I talk to her?"

"Nah. Just let her work through it. Ginny doesn't feel any differently about you, she is just surprised.

By the time they had the television working, Ginny had gotten the rest of the furniture in place and dinner was almost ready. After dinner they planned to all sit down and watch a program on the new tv.

~~~

They sat down in the living room and turned the TV set on to let it warm up. Ginny was admiring Ted's handiwork. The antenna wire went out through a hole that he had drilled in the floor and ran under the house to the pole that he and Danny had bracketed to the side
~~~

of the house. There was enough extra cord that they could move the TV if they wanted to, but it was in a neat coil behind the set. No wire showed at all, and Ginny loved how tidy it looked.

"I just wish there was a way to do something similar for the lamps."

"What do you mean?" Ted took a look around the room. There was a lamp on a small table by the telephone but that was it.

"Since I have the furniture in groupings instead of against the walls, I don't have a way to have lamps on the end tables unless I string extension cords across the floor. I thought I could maybe hide cords under rugs, but I don't have rugs yet and I'm not crazy about the idea"

Danny chimed in, "I'm not happy about that idea either, it sounds like a fire hazard."

Yes, that would be a fire hazard, and we have a way to fix it." Ted looked over the room, noting the existing electrical outlets. "I don't have all of the supplies I'd need, or I could do it tomorrow, but I could get to it next weekend."

"What are you talking about, exactly?" Danny was trying to follow where Ted was leading, but he didn't quite see it yet.

"Outlets in the floor, obviously."

"Ohhhhh. I like that!" Ginny was really interested now.

"I was under your house today. It's plenty roomy and easy to work in. I'm pretty sure I can reach up to existing wiring to tap in, or we could run a line from the fuse box. Either way, we drill the floor and drop outlet boxes in right under your tables. Easy enough."

"It doesn't sound easy to me but as long as I don't have to go under the house, I love it!"

"No, Ginny, your part is to decide how many outlets you want and where you want them. Give it some thought. You might want to move furniture someday, so try to imagine what would be the most effective in the long run."

"I will. Oh, the television is warmed up. Let's see what we have to watch!"

They tuned into a station that Ted said would be the best reception. It was an NBC station, and they got it on just in time for a program called, "The Show of Shows". It was like a series of short, funny plays and for the next half hour the three of them laughed until their sides ached.

When the program ended, Ginny turned off the set. "Ted, that was so much fun! Thank you for installing the set for us. It's just marvelous!"

Ted beamed. "It was my pleasure, Ginny. And thank you for letting me part of your inaugural session. I hope I will be invited to more nights like this, it was fun."

"If you are installing my outlets next week, I think we could provide 'dinner and a show'."

"We may have to put you on retainer, Ted. Homeownership is not for the faint of heart. My list of things to do is growing by the day."

"Danny, you know I'm always glad to help."

"Thanks, Ted, you're a good friend."

Danny walked Ted to his car and told him he would call him this week about the supplies they would need to do the electric work next weekend.

Ginny was working on the dinner dishes when he came back in, so he grabbed a towel and started putting things away. He and Ginny talked about how well the day had gone and how beautiful the house looked. There were things they still wanted to get, a few scatter rugs, some bookshelves maybe, but the house was coming together nicely.

"So, can we quit spending now? I want to see the savings account going back up."

"Yes, Ginny, we won't make any more big purchases. After I buy the supplies for the outlets, that is."

"Naturally. But that won't be much, will it?"

"No, it's not a big job. I think Ted is looking forward to the excuse to come out again."

"He is welcome anytime; he doesn't have to have an excuse."

"I'll be sure to tell him you said that."

"If those dishes get dry, I suppose we could go admire how the new sheets fit on the new bed."

"I have been looking forward to that!"

"Then here, let me grab a towel and help you along."

# 18

# Murphy's Law

Things really were going smoothly. Ginny was still worried about money, but Danny was right, the payments for the car and the house and even the furniture were all within the monthly budget and if they were careful, they could start replacing the money they had used from savings.

It was mid-December that Ginny woke up feeling nauseated and breakfast looked unappealing. She and Danny had been decorating a Christmas tree the night before. This year she had picked out a live evergreen in a pot for their tree and she planned to plant it by the driveway when they were done with it. She hoped to start that tradition and line the driveway with Christmas trees, instead of discarding them every year. The house was filled with the smell of pine and Ginny thought maybe that was making her feel sick. As the day wore on, she felt better, and the pine smell didn't bother her at all that evening. The next morning, she couldn't eat her breakfast again. Danny was concerned, but she told him her theory about the pine smell.

"It seems odd that it didn't bother you last night."

"I thought so, too, but maybe it's because we hadn't been in the house all day. There are no pine trees in the office, just the big aluminum monstrosity in the lobby." Ginny wasn't a fan of the artificial tree, but no one had asked her opinion when they brought it in.

Just like the day before, Ginny went to work and felt fine all day. When she woke up queasy the third morning, she started to realize what might be happening. She forced down some of her breakfast so that Danny wouldn't be concerned and drove them both into work.

As soon as she got to the office, she called her doctor's office and made an appointment to go there at noon for a test. She took her lunch with her and ate her sandwich in the car on the way to the doctor's office. She gave them a sample for the test and the nurse informed her they would have results in twenty four hours. She wouldn't be at home the next day and she didn't want them to call the office, so she asked if she could just call them the next afternoon.

"That would be fine Mrs. Armbruster, I will leave your results with our receptionist and tell her to expect your call."

That evening she tried to behave normally, there was no reason to bother Danny unless, she was sure. He noticed she was fidgety and picked at her supper. He even offered to take the tree out if it was bothering her.

"No, Danny, I don't think it's the tree. I'm just feeling a bit off."

"Maybe you should all Doctor Johnson tomorrow if you don't feel better. You need to eat."

"Ok, Danny, I *promise* I will call Doctor Johnson's office tomorrow."

The next day, she tried to wait until two o'clock to call the Doctor's office. She tried to get absorbed in the contracts she was typing and forget everything else, but she kept looking at the clock. At one-thirty she couldn't take it anymore.

"Hello, this is Ginny Armbruster, I'm calling for test results."

"Oh! Congratulations Mrs. Armbruster! The test was positive. Now, Doctor Johnson asked that we set an appointment for you sometime next week. Can I schedule that for you, now?"

"No, I'm afraid I'll have to call you back when I have my calendar. Thank you."

Ginny hung up the phone and stared at her typewriter. She was pregnant! How in the world...well she knew how, of course, but why now!? Her savings were at the lowest point they had been in years! They had splurged on the car, the TV, the furniture, as if the house wasn't enough. The hubris. That's what it was, hubris. Thinking that because things were going well that they always would. Like Ginny didn't know better than that.

She blamed Danny. He had talked her into spending all that money. He said they didn't need to wait. This is Danny's fault!

She immediately knew that wasn't fair. She was glad he wasn't here and that she hadn't really said any of that to him. He consulted her on every expense and let her make decisions. She couldn't lay this at his feet.

Her job! She didn't know if they would even let her continue to work, if they found out. Wives and mothers were expected to stay at home. Her marriage hadn't interfered with her work and her boss was happy with her, but this might be a different story.

She made it through the rest of the day and left at five o'clock to go pick Danny up. She drove up by the door of his shop as he was walking out. He locked up the building and jumped in the car with her. She started across the parking lot and was pulling onto the highway when Danny said. "Did you call Doctor Johnson's office today?"

Ugh. She wanted to get home to have this conversation. "Yes, I spoke with the receptionist."

"Well, when do you see him?"

"I will go in next week."

"He couldn't see you this week?"

"I guess not, Danny. How was your day? Did you finish the engine you were working on?"

"Yes, and since when do you care about what engine I'm working on?"

"I care, Danny, I listen."

"Hmmm. Something is going on here, but I will wait until you are ready to talk."

"Thank you."

He crossed his arms and stared out the window in a *huff*. Not a full-on *snit* just a *huff*. Well, Ginny could deal with that. If they could just get home and get comfortable before she had to tell him. She imagined this was going to be a long talk. She had an "emergency casserole" in the freezer that Mom had made for her in case there was an evening she didn't want to cook. Bless her for that. She could put that in the oven, toss a quick salad and then sit down with Danny to talk.

When they got home, Danny went to take a shower while she got dinner started. When he came out, she was in the living room with glasses of their own grape juice and a tray of cheese and crackers.

"Dinner will be awhile, I thought we could have a chat first."

"Sounds good. Why do I feel like I'm headed for the woodshed? Have I done something wrong?"

"Not just you...No Danny you didn't do anything wrong and I'm not angry about anything."

"Ok." He waited will she gathered herself up to speak. He was starting to get worried. Was she really sick? Did she find a lump?

"Danny, I have to just say it!... I'm pregnant!"

He was silent for a minute. The words were good news, but Ginny's face didn't look like she was happy. What was he missing here

"Honey, that's wonderful news! Aren't you excited? We might be getting our own sweet boy like Alton! Or a precious little girl! What's upset you?"

"We just spent so much money."

The *money*. That was it. Of course that was it, Ginny was a worrier.

"Ginny, this isn't about money. This is about the two of us, getting a baby of our own that we can raise here in this house that we bought for our *family*."

"Of course, it's about money! I want babies, too but I remember being that child when there was no money. I remember being shuffled from grandparent to grandparent because there was no home for us. I don't want my children to go without anything."

"Whoa! You need to slow down, sweetheart. One: You are not your mother. Even faced with the same dilemma, you would make different choices. Two: We are not homeless and not likely to be. Three: Our children *will* do without some things, because I don't want to raise spoiled brats."

Ginny took a moment to let it all soak in. "Thank you. That helped. I just wish we had bought a used car or taken your mother up on her offer. And we could have waited for the TV. And the furniture! Now we need baby furniture!"

"Ginny. Let it go. It's only money, we will make more. Can we just enjoy the fact that we are having a baby?"

Ginny smiled at him. She had not for a minute today, even considered how much they had wanted this. She was so worried about the money that she hadn't taken the time to remember how much she had loved holding Alton and how badly she wanted that for herself.

"It is rather marvelous, isn't it?"

"That's my girl. And it is wonderful. Have you told anyone yet?"

She had relaxed on Danny's shoulder but now she sat straight up again. "Told anyone?", she squeaked. "I mean I wanted to tell you before anyone else, of course, but I'm not sure I'm ready to tell anyone."

"Well, why on earth not? Mom will be beside herself."

"My job! I'm afraid if they find out they will let me go."

"Oh Ginny, you do worry. They love you at work. Your boss has said many times that he couldn't run that office without you. But if they let you go, they it's their loss and good riddance I say. You could walk into any office in town and get hired the same day. But here's a question; Do you want to work, after the baby is here?"

"I hadn't considered not working. I mean we count on my income."

"I told you before, I could give myself a raise. Mark and I have been rolling profits into a savings account and some small investments, with the plan being to expand, maybe hire a few more guys. But I told you before, the money is there. Ginny, we always planned to have children. I would never let us spend money that would jeopardize our family. You still have investments, too. I know we ran our savings down but sweetie, isn't the house what we were saving for?"

"I know you're right. I've been without money. Even as a teenager, when I made money babysitting, the other girls ran right out and spent it but I couldn't. I saved it all. A good thing, to because that's how I got to Bakersfield."

"My sweet wife, I know that rough start made you who you are, so personally, I'm grateful for it, because I love everything about you. But maybe, just for now, you trust me that I am here for you. Work or don't work, whichever makes you happy. But I will always find a way to take care of you and our family, no matter what."

"My Papa would have always taken care of me."

"Your Papa did his best and didn't leave you in that mess on purpose. But I have something that your Papa doesn't. A very large life insurance policy that would make sure you never found yourself in the situation your mother was in."

"Danny, I didn't know that! Why didn't I know that?"

"It's something Mark and I agreed on when we opened the shop. He doesn't want Sheila and the kids to suffer if something happened to him. It's paid out of the business with our other coverage."

"I married a very smart man"

"I thought you knew that. Hey, something smells delicious."

"Oh. The casserole should be about done. I'll go get it."

"No, my sweet, you are going to put your feet on the coffee table and let me finish up dinner. I'll call you when it's on the table."

"Don't be silly. I'm barely pregnant. I think I can handle taking a salad out of the fridge and a casserole out of the oven."

"So can I. Just consider this practice for how you will be treated for the next 9 months."

Ginny settled into the sofa while Danny finished dinner.

"Damn, I married a good man." She murmured into glass of grape juice.

$$19$$

# Meanwhile Back at the
# Ranch

In the months since JT's stroke and Mother's somewhat hostile takeover, Chet, Greta and Mother had spent a good deal of time at her kitchen table going over ledgers and making plans.

The property itself was in good shape. Chet's work over the past several years had his forty acres with all new fences, and the two hundred acres of his mother's property was fenced and cross-fenced to allow them to move the cattle off part of it if they wanted to let the grass grow. The barn was in good condition and Chet had been cutting posts to expand the corrals. A larger herd meant they would need more room to get them in for vaccinations and the like.

Chet had found them an Angus bull with good bloodlines. He was registered with the American Angus Association as were a few of the cows and calves Chet had purchased. The idea was to slowly sell off all of the "grade" cattle and eventually get an all-registered herd. Using the bull to service his neighbors' cattle was a little income on the side, too.

Greta had come up with the idea to train calves to show at the county fairs. The more blue ribbons their cattle got, the more they would be worth. Their bull had come to them halter-trained and would lead around like a puppy, he was so gentle. A good thing, too, because he was too big to argue with!

Greta and Chet had spent every evening after supper, all summer long, putting halters on calves and walking them around the corral, making them stand pretty, rubbing their bellies with a cane when they were behaving well. They kept these calves close to the barn lot, so they could get to them every day. In September, they took four of them to the county fair and won ribbons on three of them. One first place and two second place. Not bad for the first year and next year they would enter more fairs, in neighboring counties. They had learned a lot about what makes a winner in the judges' eyes.

Chet had gotten an offer to buy the first-place winner, right there at the arena. It was a good offer and he was tempted but this little bull-calf wasn't related to their big bull and Chet had an eye on him as a replacement someday. So far, he was looking to be every bit as good a bull as the other one, but he was young yet. He would just have to wait and see.

So far, the money wasn't pouring in, it was mostly going out. But it was all there in assets. The herd was worth more every day and if that bull was worth his feed, next year's calves would be where they would see the money coming back in.

One thing Chet was working on was how to bale their own hay. They had a good tractor, they had good pasture and if they managed it right, they could get a couple of cuttings before they turned cows back on it. But he didn't have a mower or a bailer. He didn't know whether it was better to buy equipment or go in on shares with a neighbor who had equipment, meaning he would take part of the hay, or just give up and buy hay. Since figuring expenses wasn't his area, not on something like this anyway, he went to his mother to ask what she thought.

"Well Chester, that is certainly something to consider. (Gawd, he hated being called Chester)

Do you think we would have enough hay to sell, or would we use it all.?"

"I reckon that depends on how many cows we keep puttin' on this place but as it stands now, we would probably have a bit more than we could use."

"And where would we store it? In the barn?"

"Some in the barn loft and I was thinkin' I could build a hay shed off the east side of the barn. I can cut timber, and it shouldn't be hard to come up with sheet iron for the roof."

"That sounds good. I'll call Mr. Jenkins at the tractor dealership and see what equipment he has. Let me ponder on this for a day or two. But the idea has merit."

Chet couldn't believe the difference in his mother since JT's stroke. She was easier to talk to, she was making good business decisions, and she was happy. Mrs. Fleming did most of the care for JT. She helped him dress and changed his sheets. She fed him and walked him to the makeshift water closet they had set up for him behind a screen. It wasn't an ideal situation, but it was better than a bed pan. Mrs. Fleming also helped around the house anytime she wasn't busy with JT. When school started again, Mother would come home to dinner already cooking on the stove and the house neat as a pin.

Mother only dropped in once a day to ask JT if he needed anything and give him a report on what was being done on the farm. He was still quietly furious at her high-handed decision making, and it made him more furious that her changes seemed to be successful, but he couldn't exactly complain to anyone, since she kept him informed and wasn't spending his money. But someday, he would get out of this bed and wipe the smug smile off of her face.

Mother talked to the other teachers and her church ladies and boohooed and carried on about her poor JT and how she was trying her best to keep the farm running for him with Chet's help. They all sympathized with her hard plight and told her how strong and wonderful she was. Chet saw all of this, and the thing was, he was pretty sure his mother believed everything she was saying. He had seen it before. She wanted the world to be a nice place, and she just blocked out anything that was unpleasant. Now that she had JT under control, she would just pretend everything had always been hunky-dory.

For once, it didn't bother Chet. The change in her was so big he didn't care what she had to tell herself. She was even being nicer to Greta, listening to her ideas for the cattle and letting her help with the ledgers. Of course she couldn't get enough of Alton, but that wasn't new. She still drove Chet crazy, but not as much as she used to.

Chet and Greta had started talking about maybe building another room onto the cabin. Greta was ready to do it now, but Chet still had ideas of building up on the hill. He didn't know how he felt about working more on the cabin when he could be getting ready to build a real house.

Greta had other ideas. "Chet, I know you do what you think is best and I love you for it, but could you listen to what *I* want? I love this house. I want a little more room, yeah, but I don't even know if I want a big house on the hill, not yet. I have worked hard on making the yard look nice. This is *our* home."

"But wouldn't you like to draw up a plan for a house just the way you like it? Have a bathroom and hot water and real bedrooms?"

"Some of those things sound nice, but why can't we have them here?"

"We could, but that place on top of the hill has such a pretty view. A house up there would be like we were on top of the world."

"Yeah, and down here in the holler, the wind and storms just sort of pass us by. I feel safe, tucked in down here."

"Well, you do have a point there."

"I ain't saying that we could never build a house up there, if you got your heart set on it, but I just want to raise our babies here."

"Well so far there is just the one baby and I'm not sure he cares."

"*I* care! And it ain't just one baby, not for long anyway."

"What are you saying? Greta, are you expecting again?"

"I think I am, I was trying not to say anything until I was sure. But I don't want to think about building a house and moving everything with two babies. We have so much going on now with the extra farm chores and training calves and I just don't want to think about building a big house. I just want a bedroom!" Greta was very near tears by the end of her tirade.

Chet was smiling. When Greta saw him, she looked around for something to throw at him. "What are you smiling at?"

"Well, you are so darned adorable it makes me giggle sometimes, and you just told me we are having another baby, so I feel like I have a lot to smile about."

"I told you I'm not sure."

"Oh, I think you're pretty sure. You have been giving it some thought, haven't you?"

"Well yeah, I think I probably am, but I need to go see Doctor Jeffries to be sure."

"We will get you in to see Doctor Jeffries as soon as we can. And if you want a bedroom, I'll build you one."

"Thank you, Chet, for understanding."

By Christmastime, the new additions to the house had been started, Chet got Dave Bishop to pour concrete before the weather got too cold, and Chet was working on the frame a little every day. All Greta wanted was a bedroom of their own, but Chet had other ideas. If they were staying in this house, he wanted to do it right. He was adding a bedroom, a bathroom and an area by the back door where he could put a water heater and maybe a washing machine someday and room for Greta to have a sewing machine.

Greta was indeed expecting, and they had told everyone now. Greta had written a Christmas card to Ginny and Danny to tell them, and on the day she mailed it, she got a letter from Ginny saying she was pregnant. Ginny wasn't very far along, or she didn't think so anyway. She was seeing her doctor that week and hadn't told anyone yet. She wanted to tell Greta and said it was ok to tell Chet, but maybe not tell Mother, yet. She wrote to Greta about how worried she was that she would lose her job, but that Danny said they would be ok.

Ginny was expecting, too. It sounded like maybe Greta was a little further along, but their babies would be very close in age. Greta thought that was just wonderful.

Greta told Chet but asked him not to tell Mother. Chet nodded and said, "I expect she would like to tell her that herself, when she is ready." Mother was thrilled that Greta was pregnant, she would be over the moon when she heard about Ginny.

Christmas came and Chet surprised Greta with a used Singer sewing machine. It was an electric machine! Greta had only ever used her Ma's treadle machine and was excited to try it! Chet told her he would get her sewing room ready to use just as soon as he possibly could. Alton was amazed at all the fun! The Christmas trees and the cookies and the presents! He had everyone laughing, even JT!

Alton would climb up on JT's bed and say, "Papa", making JT smile. JT still called him 'Jim-boy' which Greta hated but it didn't seem to catch on with anyone else. JT had asked for Greta to buy Alton a teddy bear from him and when Alton visited him Christmas day he gave it to him. From then on Monkey had a new friend and they both went with Alton everywhere.

In January Ginny finally called her mother to tell her the good news about the baby. As expected, Mother was tickled pink. She offered to come stay with Ginny and Danny to help when the baby came but Ginny (quietly horrified at the idea) told her they would be just fine with help from Danny's mom and that she was sure Greta would need her there to help with two babies. Ginny made a note to herself to make that up to Greta somehow.

JT was making progress. His speech was less slurred, and he could move his left leg a little more. One day in February he had a very good day. He sat up in his recliner and played with Alton and he said he felt better than he had in months. That night there was a loud crash and both Mother and Mrs. Fleming came running. The crash was a pitcher from JT's nightstand. JT was sideways across his bed, his sheets and blankets wound around him. He was barely breathing. Mother called for an ambulance and Doctor Jeffries, while Mrs. Fleming stayed with JT and tried to straighten out the bedclothes and get him in a more comfortable position. Then they waited for help to arrive. Mother held JT's hand and spoke softly to him about the farm and baby Alton. He looked at her and seemed to understand but he wasn't able to talk.

Doctor Jeffries arrived just before the ambulance. He listened to JT's heart and lungs and gave him a quick examination. When the ambulance attendants arrived with the stretcher, he waved them off. He asked them to wait in the next room while he finished his examination. As Mother and Mrs. Fleming looked on, he listened carefully to JT's heart for another minute. He reached to close JT's eyes and looked at his watch. He scribbled a note for himself and then turned to Mother. "Mrs. Smith, I'm afraid he has passed."

Mother dropped into the recliner and put her face in her hands. "I don't understand. He was doing so well, just earlier today he said he felt better than he had in months."

"I've seen that before. Sometimes when I person has been sick for as long as Mr. Smith was, they will rally a bit before they pass. I don't know if the exertion is too much or maybe it's God's way of giving them a good last day. But, as much as he wanted to, Mr. Smith was never going to recover from that stroke. There was just too much damage. It's only because of the excellent care that you and Mrs. Fleming have given him that he was as comfortable as he had been for these last months.

"That was all Mrs. Fleming. She has been a Godsend."

Mrs. Fleming spoke, "It has been my pleasure to help you here ma'am. I've been happy with your family."

Doctor Jeffries gave the ladies a moment of privacy and then he led the attendants in with the stretcher. He escorted the women out to the living room while the men did their work. There would be no need for the hospital, they would transport Mr. Smith straight to the funeral parlor in Grove.

The next morning Mother called Chet and told him. She asked him if he would give her a ride to Grove to meet with the funeral director. He and Greta came over right away. Mrs. Fleming had bundled all of the bedding to be washed and had wiped the entire room with Lysol. She would arrange for the bed to be removed as soon as she could.

Alton went into JT's room and turned back to the living room, confused and scared. He ran to his mommy, saying, "Papa?" It broke Greta's heart. JT may not have been everyone's cup of tea, but he was good to Alton and the little boy was going to miss him. Greta had no idea how to explain this to a little boy that wasn't even two years old.

Mother took Alton and sat with him in the big rocker. "Alton, your Papa has gone to live with Jesus." Chet made a scoffing noise, and his mother glared at him. "Jesus is taking care of Papa' so he isn't sick anymore. We won't be able to see him anymore, but Papa is happy, is that ok?"

"Papa happy?" asked Alton his bright eyes showing how he was taking in Grandmother's words.

"Yes, 'Papa' is happy."

"Ok." With that Alton climbed down and went to find Monkey and Bear.

"He took that well," said Greta, surprised.

"Children are accepting if you explain things to them. I wish I had known that sooner. It wasn't until I started teaching that I realized that little minds can grasp more than we give them credit for."

Chet's ears perked up. That was the nearest he had ever heard his mother come to admitting that she might have made mistakes. He knew better than to push it though. She would just dismiss him and say, "I don't know what you could be referring to." Her memory became very spotty when it came to anything she didn't care to remember.

Before they left for the funeral parlor, Mother placed a person-to-person call to Ginny's office in Bakersfield. It was the most expensive way to call, but the charges wouldn't start until the operator had Ginny on the phone. Mother didn't plan to stay on the phone long.

"Mother?" Ginny's voice came on the phone.

"Yes, Ginny, hello."

"Mother, what's wrong?"

"I wanted to let you know that JT passed away last night."

"Oh Mother, I'm sorry."

"Chet and I will be heading to the funeral home to make arrangements as soon as we finish our call."

"Will you want me to be there for the service, Mother? I'll need time to make travel arrangements."

"Oh, Heaven's no Ginny! I wouldn't think of having you travel in your delicate condition! No, no not at all!"

"Mother, I'm pregnant not sick."

"Ginny, you must take care of yourself! Losing a child is not something I would ever want you to go through."

Ginny remembered Mother's still-born child. It was her only pregnancy from her marriage with JT and though it was never mentioned, Ginny was sure it had been hard on her mother. She understood that more now than ever.

"Yes, Mother I will take care of myself. Please, write and let me know how I can help you. I'm very sorry to hear your news."

"Thank you, Ginny, I'll write." With that she hung up the phone.

She and Chet went to the funeral home and since Mrs. Fleming didn't need her assistance, Greta went home with Alton. She called her mother to tell her the news. Ma said she would tell Daddy and the boys. She said Bill would probably come over to see if Chet needed anything later today.

"That would probably be good, Ma. Chet's relationship with JT was...complicated."

"I know honey. Stepparents are rarely welcomed, and JT Smith was a hard man to love. I can't imagine the circumstances that brought those two together as man and wife, but I'm sure there is a story."

"I guess I never thought about it."

"Oh, you young people always forget that your parents were once young, too. We had feelings and made mistakes. Here's a secret, we still do."

"I know, Ma." But Greta was a little ashamed of herself because she hadn't thought of it that way. Is that the way of it? Would Alton just think that she and Chet had all the answers? That they never loved or laughed or were silly kids together. She had never thought of her Ma as young, but that was crazy. She was barely over forty now. Chet's mother was older, and JT had been a good deal older than her, but none of them were ancient. She felt a little self-absorbed that she had never thought of them as *people*.

She hung up the phone and spent a little time on the floor with Alton, playing with Monkey and Bear. She hoped that no matter what Alton thought of her when he was grown, that at least he would always know she loved him. She could say that for her Ma and Daddy, she had always felt safe and loved.

Chet and his mother returned from town, and Chet dropped Mother at her house, promising to return in a little while with Greta and Alton. Greta heard his truck coming up the road and was waiting for him on the front porch. "How did it go?"

"Everything went just fine. I told her we would come right back so we can talk about things. The funeral will be tomorrow morning though."

"Tomorrow? That soon?"

"No reason to wait, JT doesn't have any folks to come here and the men from his lodge and the people from their church can all be told today. The church ladies are calling each other now. Every day he sits in the funeral home costs more, so Mother just wanted to get it done. He already owned a burial plot."

"He did?"

"Yeah, when we first moved here, he bought four spaces in the Starkville cemetery for the two of them and me and Ginny. Like we would ever want to be planted next to him. I think he only did it to show off to his lodge brothers that he was a family man and belonged to the community. JT was always bout looking good."

Alton was just waking up from his nap, so Ginny changed him and grabbed Monkey and Bear and hefted him on to her hip to make the walk.

"Here let's just take the truck. You don't need to be carrying him everywhere."

"You could carry him, ya know."

"Woman, just get in the truck," Chet grinned and opened the door for her.

"Oh. Ma said Bill would be over later. She thought you might need some help with chores."

"I appreciate it. I am running behind."

Back at Mother's house they went in through the kitchen door and found Mother and Mrs. Fleming in what looked at first like an argument. Both women were teary-eyed and red in the face, Greta said, "What on earth is going on here?"

"I came home and found that not only had Mrs. Fleming done all the laundry and called the men to remove the bed and cleaned everything in sight, but after searching the house for her I found her in the attic. The mad woman was packing her bags to leave."

"What?!" Geta and Chet cried together.

"That's what I said. What is this?"

"I was hired to take care of Mr. Smith." Mrs. Fleming wrung her hands and looked very uncomfortable.

"You said just last night that you were happy here."

"I have been happy here. But in other homes, once there was no one to care for I was asked to leave."

"Well, I don't remember doing the asking."

"I just thought..."

"Well, you thought wrong. Chester and I were going to talk to you and Greta about some things. I didn't think you would be gone before I got the chance."

"I would not have left without saying goodbye."

"Well, that's good to know at least."

Chet put his hand on his mother's shoulder and walked her over to the kitchen table. "Let's all sit down, Mrs. Fleming, you, too."

Greta settled Alton into his play cubby in the old fireplace and he was showing Monkey and Bear how to stack blocks. She sat by Chet and waited to see what it was they wanted to talk about.

Mother began, "We started at the funeral home and made arrangements for a simple ceremony to be held there in the morning and a graveside service to follow. The ladies at the church will oversee a potluck lunch in the church basement so folks don't feel like they have to drive out here to visit afterwards. We will have to be there for a good while to let everyone pay their respects."

"That sounds fine." Greta nodded and Mother went on, "We went to the bank next and checked the safety deposit box and talked to Mr. Schumaker, the bank president. He is a lodge brother of JT's hand was fairly sure of the state of things as far as a will. The property and all the bank accounts were held in both of our names, so there was no need for a will. I have what is called 'right of survivorship' as his widow. Mr. Schumaker said that he had discussed this with JT in the past and unless something had occurred that he was unaware of, JT didn't make a will. Since we didn't find one in the safe deposit box, we think that's true. Except for personal items everything was already in my name."

"We did find a small life insurance policy that I was unaware of. Not much but enough to cover his funeral and all with maybe a few dollars left. But what we found that surprised us was several hundred dollars' worth of US Savings Bonds made out in Alton's name. I guess JT did have someone he wanted to leave something to."

Greta rocked back in her chair. "What does that even mean?"

"It means that if Alton lets them mature, they are twenty-year bonds, he will have a pretty good nest egg to start out on."

"Well, I'll be." Greta looked over at her little boy who was, as of now, wealthier than she had ever been. "I'll be."

"I know how you feel honey." Mother patted Greta's hand. "There was one person he cared about."

"But now for you, Mrs. Fleming. You are not being held here against your will, so if you want to leave you may, but I wish you would consider staying on."

"I would love to stay. I don't really have anywhere to go other than staying with my daughter, but I didn't think you would need me here."

"It has been a blessing to have you here. With me teaching and now how we are expanding the cattle business, I'm quite busy. And also, I would rather have the company, than to be alone here."

"Then I will be happy to stay."

Both women looked pleased with their deal.

# 20

# Greta

The funeral went as planned. There was a fair turnout at the service at the funeral home but only a few at the graveside. But there was a surprisingly large turnout at the reception at the church. JT's lodge brothers were all there, most of the teachers from Starkville school, all the Reddington family and members of the church. Chet watched his mother graciously accept their condolences and heard her talk about what a wonderful husband JT had been. She had never been happy as a wife, if she could be happy as a widow he wouldn't spoil it for her.

He couldn't get over what JT had done for Alton. He had always made it a point that Chet and Ginny were not his children, yet he had put money away for Alton. Money that Mother had apparently not known about. Chet had never understood JT and now he guessed he never would.

Ginny chased a rowdy little toddler from the service to the graveside and now at the church. Thank Heavens, Ma had come to the church. She was holding on to Alton while Greta took a seat. "You should get Chet to take you home honey, you look tired."

"I am tired, but he needs to stay with his mother until she is ready to go, and I can't ask her to cut it short."

"Well Bill can take you then." She waved for Bill to come to her. "Brother, you need to take Greta and Alton home. She needs rest."

"I can't just disappear, Ma."

"Then go tell Chet you are leaving. I'll hold Alton."

"Is it ok with you Bill?"

"Oh, heck yeah. I'm ready to go."

"Watch your cheeky mouth in the house of the lord, son. But thank you for driving Sister home."

Greta approached Chet and tapped him on the shoulder.

"Hey honey, you ok?"

"Alton and I are both getting tired. Bill said he could take us home."

"I'm sorry, I should be paying better attention to you."

"It's ok, you mother needs you today. Bill can take us."

"Ok, I'll be home as soon as I can."

Bill carried Alton out to the truck and helped Greta in. "You do look rough, Sis."

"Thanks a lot! But I am tired. The last two days have been hard."

Bill got Greta and Alton in the house and offered to go do some chores for Chet. He knew his way around Chet's farm, he could do about anything Chet could.

Greta said, "I should go. We need to lead those calves; we missed last night."

"Later Sis, you need a nap and so does Alton." Greta didn't feel like arguing so she curled up around Alton, Monkey and Bear on her bed. Bill waited to make sure she was asleep and went out to turn water on to the stock tank in the corral.

He came back a few minutes later and Greta was asleep, but she was groaning and tossing a little. He picked up baby Alton and carried him to his crib. He came back and watched Greta for a few minutes, and something just didn't seem right. Everyone he knew was at the church. He didn't know who to call. He felt a little foolish, but he figured he would rather feel foolish than make a big mistake, so he looked up Doctor Jeffries' number and called. Fortunately, Doctor Jeffries had returned to his office after the funeral home, so he was in.

"Doctor Jeffries, this is Bill, Greta Masters' brother. I just brought Greta home because she was tired and she's asleep but she's moaning and tossing, and she feels a little warm. She just doesn't seem right."

"It's probably nothing but just being worn out but I'll come by and check on her. You keep her covered and if she wakes up tell her to stay in bed. I don't want her up until I've checked on her, ok?"

"Ok Doctor, I will."

He hung up the phone and was glad the doctor was coming out but also a little scared. He said it was probably nothing, but he also said he didn't want her up. He covered her up with a blanket and sat by her to wait.

The doctor pulled his car right up to the door. He grabbed his bag and came right in. He didn't look like he thought it was nothing.

"Greta, it's Doc Jeffries, can you hear me?"

"Mmmm Doc? Why are you here? Is Alton ok?"

"Yes, Greta, he's fine. How are you feeling?"

"I'm fine, just tired."

"How does your tummy feel Greta?"

"Mmmm. Sore. Kinda achy."

"Bill, could you step out for a few minutes so I could examine Greta?"

"Yeah sure."

Bill stepped out on the porch and paced, waiting for Doctor Jeffries to call him back in. He heard Chet's truck coming up from the creek. He was so relieved he could cry. He didn't, but he could've.

Chet jumped out of the car before the truck stopped rolling, "Why is Doctor Jeffrie's car here?"

Bill had to practically tackle him to keep him from going into the house. "He's lookin' at Greta. He said it was probably nothin', but he told me to wait outside."

Chet calmed himself down, but he took up pacing where Bill had left off.

Before long Doctor Jeffries opened the front door and asked them to come in. Greta was propped up on pillows, still looking tired but wide awake now.

"What's going on Doctor, is Greta, ok?"

"I think she will be Chet but the next few days are important. Greta is halfway through this pregnancy. She hasn't gained as much weight as I would like to see at this stage, and I think I see some signs of anemia. She needs to eat beef, liver if you can. For the next week I don't want you out of this bed except to go to the privy. I will check on her again, then we will decide what comes next. For the rest of this pregnancy, no training calves, no carrying Alton or even picking him up. Even if I take her off full bed rest, she needs to spend as much time with her feet up as she can. Not standing at the sink or stove. Do you hear me, Greta?"

"Yes Doctor, but I just don't see how..."

"Greta, I fear for this pregnancy. I don't want to scare you, but you are stubborn and won't listen to me if it's about your health. I need you to understand that this baby is in danger if you don't follow my instructions to the letter."

"She's going to listen Doctor; I'm making sure of that." Chet stepped over to take Greta's hand. "I have a question, if she isn't supposed to be walking, isn't he walk to the outhouse going to be too far?'

"It isn't ideal, but I don't want her squatting over a jug either."

"What about the set-up we had for JT, with the chair and screen?"

"That would be good, I should have thought of that."

Greta spoke up, "Chet I would rather just walk to the privy, I'll go slow."

"Greta you will not walk if it isn't safe! It's the chair or I'm carrying to the privy."

With three men glaring at her, Greta gave in. She really did want to take care of herself for the baby, but using the bathroom in her living room sounded horrible.

"I have an idea. If you can put up with the screen for a few days, I can do better. He turned to Doctor Jeffries, "We are building on a bedroom and bathroom. It isn't nearly done yet, but I could get the bathroom area cleared out and set the chair and screen in there. I could have walls on there in a couple of days."

"That is a good idea. It's a lot shorter walk than the outhouse. Just make sure there is nothing she will trip on."

"I can walk! I may need rest, but I haven't lost my legs!"

"Ok that's fair, just be careful. We can't have you falling down."

Bill and Chet walked Doctor Jeffries out to his car. He asked Chet to call him if he noticed any changes that he was worried about and said he would be back next week.

Bill went to start some chores while Chet went to talk to Greta. When he went in, she was wiping tears off of her face. Chet sat beside her and held her hands. "Greta, what can I do?"

"I'm just so sorry Chet, I let you down again. First, I couldn't feed Alton and now I can't even take care of this baby that isn't even born yet!"

Chet heard Aton waking up and went to get him. "He put him on the bed beside Greta and said, "Here Buddy, I think your mommy needs a hug." Alton crawled up and planted a wet kiss on Greta's cheek and laid his head on her shoulder. "He patted her, saying, "It's ok, it's ok." Just like she said when he had an owie. It made her laugh.

"There that's better." Chet sat on the bed again. "Now, how is it that you keep thinking you let me down? Look how perfect our little boy is. And you're going to have another beautiful baby for us in a few months. Your only job is to make yourself and that baby healthy. That's all, and I'll be a happy man."

"But that ain't my only job Chet and you know it. Who is going to cook and wash dishes and take care of Alton and do the laundry and…I can't even train those calves now."

"I can cook and wash the dishes. Heck, I'm a better cook than you are anyway."

Greta punched him in the arm. "That ain't nice! It may be true but not nice."

Alton glared at Chet, "Not nice!"

Greta and Chet both laughed. Greta hugged Alton, "Mommy was teasing. Daddy is being really nice. We love Daddy.

"Wuv Daddy."

"I'm going to have to start watching what I say." Chet ruffled Alton's hair.

"We both are."

Chet changed Alton's diaper and got him settled to play with toys in his room. Greta could see him playing from the bed. "I'm headed out to help Bill with the chores. Alton will be fine and don't you dare pick him up. If you need me, ring the dinner bell. I'll be listening. Call Mother if you need to, but don't pick him up."

"Ok, ok, I'll be good. Is your mother home?"

"She should be, Mrs. Flemimg was driving her home, and they were packing up food to bring home when I left. I'll drop by after chores and see if there is a spare casserole. I don't know why folks think she needs so much food."

"They just don't know what else to do."

"Reckon so. I'll be back as soon as I can." He kissed her on the forehead and headed out.

He caught up with Bill at the barn lot. He was looking pale himself. "Hey Bill, you ok?

"Honestly, Chet, I was scared to death. Greta looked bad but she didn't seem sick like anything I ever saw. I didn't know what to do."

"Well, you did fine. I'm sorry I wasn't here. But I'm glad you were."

"I can be here more if your gonna need help."

"I may at that. Can Earl spare you from your place."

"He can if it's for Greta. Daddy's girl you know."

After they got chores done, Chet sent Bill to check on Greta while he stopped at his mother's to let her know what was going on. He told her and Mrs. Flemimg what the doctor had said.

Mother said, "Well I feel like a fool. I told Ginny not to come and take care of herself and then let Greta get over stressed, right under my nose."

"Well, I guess we all missed it. Greta acts so tough, but the truth is, she is a tiny little thing, and she works too hard. She totes Alton every-where, she hauls feed sacks and hay, she pushes those calves around, she is just doing too much, especially while she is pregnant."

"You're right, we need to quit working her like a field hand. She is a wife and mother."

"For tonight, I was wondering if there is a casserole or something I could take for dinner. And maybe some beef bouillon you have any. Doctor says she needs beef to build her up."

"I can get that for you. We have more food than we can eat in a month. We were wrapping things to go in the deep freeze."

Mrs. Fleming selected a casserole that looked like it had some meat and cheese in it. She found some bouillon cubes and put them with the casserole in a cardboard box. She reached up on top of the refrig-erator and took down a tin. It was filled with waxed paper pouches of tea. She selected one and put it in the box. "Make Greta a tea with a tablespoon of this in a cup of hot water, let it steep for ten minutes. Have her drink it morning and night. It's red raspberry leaf. It will help strengthen her womb."

Mother nodded at Chet. He took the box from Mrs. Flemimg and thanked her.

"I will be over tomorrow to help at your house and watch Alton for a while. If it's ok, with Mrs. Smith that is."

"Yes, Mrs. Fleming, I think that is a fine idea."

"Thank ya both. I best be getting back to Greta. I sent Bill to her, but he was pretty shook up."

"The poor boy. He did well to get her home and call for help, while we are all otherwise occupied." Mother said as she walked Chet to the door. "Give Greta my love."

"I will. Goodnight."

Back at the house, Chet talked Bill into going on home for the night. He offered to make himself a pallet on the floor in Alton's room in case they needed him. The truth was he knew there was nothing for him to do, he was just having trouble leaving Greta. Chet convinced him that he would need him to help with chores in the evening more than anything else, besides, no one had told Greta's folks anything yet. It would be better for Bill to go explain in person than for Chet and Greta to try and talk to them on the phone. He could do more to convince them that all was under control.

After Bill left, Chet had the casserole in the oven and Greta was sipping her beef bouillon. He had her tea brewing for her to drink with dinner. He pulled a comfy chair over by the bed to sit with her for a few minutes.

"Chet, there is something you don't know. I asked Doctor Jeffries to let me tell you myself and I didn't want Bill to know or for Alton to hear, since he repeats everything." They both looked over at Alton who was pushing a toy truck around his room and not paying any attention to the grown-ups.

"What is that, hon?"

When Doctor Jeffries checked me, I was bleedin' a little. Just a little. But that's why he doesn't want me walkin' or squattin' over the pot. He said it could stop but to be very careful not to do anything to make it worse. Walking to the bathroom is ok as long as I don't carry anything or bend over or nuthin'."

She started to tear up and Chet reached over to put his arm around her. "That don't change nuthin'. Doc told us what to do and we are going to do it. Mrs. Fleming is even going to come during the days and help with Alton and do some cleaning. You have a housekeeper, ain't that fancy?"

She smiled. "I guess I am a real lady of leisure. I will 'sit on a pillow and sew a fine seam'. Actually, that's not a bad idea. If we could get baby patterns cut out of that flannel material, I could sit, and hand sew to keep from going crazy."

"I bet mother would loan you some of her Reader's Digest Books to read, too."

"This might be a bad idea. I might start likin' layin' in bed all day."

"I think it's just fine. Now I'm gonna get that dinner for us."

Chet brought out a folding table and set it up by the bed. He put Alton's highchair beside it and pulled the comfy chair back and brought a kitchen chair in. He set plates on the table and put a trivet in the middle for the casserole. After he got Alton in has highchair, he carefully carried the hot casserole dish and put it on the table. He gave Greta her tea and poured himself a coffee and a milk for Alton. Greta watched it all, fighting herself not to get up and help. Jokes aside, it was against her nature to be waited on. This wasn't going to be easy.

# 21

# Mom

Ginny was able to get Danny to wait until she had seen her doctor before he told his mom. But just barely, he was very excited. She saw Doctor Johnson and he confirmed that she was about eight or nine weeks pregnant. Early days yet, but he saw no reason for concern, she was a healthy young woman.

"Can I keep my job?"

"Considering the work you do; I see no reason why not. I would say right now, continue doing anything you are used to doing; I wouldn't take up any new, strenuous hobbies, but just let your body guide you. If you feel tired, take a nap. If you are hungry, eat. As long as your cravings are for food, then let them guide you. If you crave anything that isn't food, call my office, that can be a sign of a deficiency. Otherwise, if there are no problems, just come see me next month."

"How long do you think, I will be able to work?"

"As long as you feel fine, I think you could work up until your last month. But we can discuss that as we go along. If you get any swelling or other problems, we may need you to take time off. We can cross that bridge, *if* we come to it."

That night when she picked up Danny, they drove to his mom's house. She barely got the car stopped before he was out and running up the front steps. He waited for Ginny to catch up and then banged on the front door. He heard Mom coming to the door, "Yes, who is it?"

"Mom, it's Danny and Ginny!" Mom opened the door, and Danny scooped her up in a hug. Ginny managed to get in and close the door while he twirled his mom around.

"Danny, what in the world?"

Ginny said, "Let's go into the living room and sit down maybe, Danny if you can let your mother walk!"

They settled in, Ginny and Danny on the sofa, Mom in her chair. "Now tell me what is going on."

"Ginny's pregnant!" Danny just blurted it out, he couldn't contain himself.

"Oh, how wonderful! Ginny, I'm so pleased. How are you feeling."

"A little nausea in the morning, but it goes away by lunch. Other than that, I feel great."

"That's good. The old wives would say that morning sickness is a sign that the pregnancy is strong."

"I hadn't heard that, but I'll look at it as a good sign."

"Mom, Danny said, "We haven't told anyone but you. It's early yet and Ginny doesn't want to rock the boat at work."

"You plan to keep working, then?"

"Yes."

"Danny you are fine with that?"

"Of course, Mom. Ginny likes her work."

"What about when there is a baby to care for? I don't expect they will let you bring a baby to the office."

"No, I'm not even sure they will let me once I start showing, but I hope they will. I will take some time off once the baby is born, but I will have to find out if they will hold my job for me. If not, I guess I'll start over somewhere else."

"Who will take care of the baby, then?"

"Mom, we haven't figured everything out, but we will. Maybe we will hire help."

"That makes no sense. Go back to work so you can give your pay-check to a stranger taking care of the baby."

Mom was getting worked up and was making Ginny anxious. She hadn't expected things to go this way.

"Mom, I told you we haven't thought about it yet. You're upsetting Ginny. Can't we just be happy?"

"I'm so sorry Ginny, and yes Danny, you are right. This is a joyous occasion, and I couldn't be more pleased. I let my worry get away from me. I know Ginny doesn't have family here and I just want the baby to have the best."

"Well, we hadn't talked about it, but if I remodeled that small apartment behind the garage, we could offer someone a place to live as part of wages for babysitting. I'm sure if we asked around that some-one knows a trustworthy person."

"Hmmm. Well, I guess there is time to think on it. Now will you stay to supper. I have chicken in the oven and it's more than I need. We can celebrate!"

Ginny was relieved that the conversation was back on track. They did stay for supper and Danny went to help Mom in the kitchen while they both made Ginny promise to put her feet up. She didn't hate be-ing spoiled a little. She was feeling tired.

Mom had given Ginny a lot to think about. She had been worrying about keeping her job and hadn't given much thought to who would care for the baby. The girls that she knew from school who married and had babies had all quit working. Was she a bad mother if she didn't? She had always resented her mother for leaving her and Chet, but she was gone for months at a time. When they lived together, and mother was teaching, she never thought anything of it but of course they had been in school by then. Was she just a bad person, that she would rather work than stay home? She and Danny shared chores and their house was clean, they cooked meals and packed their lunches for work. What would she even do at home all day? With a baby she would be busy, but she still just couldn't picture it.

On the drive home, she asked Danny what he thought about hiring a person to take care of the baby. He was driving and she was leaning against the passenger door facing him. She saw him thinking it over before he answered. "Ya know, Ginny, we really haven't had time to plan, but I fell a bit caught off guard that I hadn't thought about it."

"Me too! It seems like we should have realized that someone would have to be with the baby."

"You know if we didn't find someone to live-in a bet Mom would love to play Grandma if we brought the baby to her every day."

"Ugh. I mean it's not a bad idea, but it would mean dropping you off, driving to your mom's house and getting out with a baby and whatever paraphernalia is required for the day and then the drive to the office. It would add a half hour to the commute."

"Ugh is right, I hadn't thought of that. Ok, we will keep thinking."

On Saturday, Ginny and Danny were puttering around the house, getting things done from their endless 'to do' list when the telephone rang. Danny answered and Ginny heard him say, "Hello Mom, what's up? Sure, we are home all day. That sounds fine. See you then."

"Your mom is coming?"

"Yeah, she said she wanted to drop some things off."

"Ok, that sounds good. An excuse to stop finding more work to do," she grinned. "I'll go change."

"Oh, I see how it is, any excuse to get out of cleaning baseboards."

"You bet," she said and threw her dust cloth at him before she skittered to the bedroom to change clothes.

Ginny made a tray of snacks and opened another bottle of their grape juice and set out glasses. Mom arrived and had Danny help her carry in a few things from the car.

"I brought you some Christmas ornaments that I thought you might like, just a few small things that Danny's grandmother made."

"Oh, how sweet. These are going right on the tree. They are beautiful."

She opened the other carton that she had brought. "These are some of Danny's baby things. Just a few little items; First this is the baby book I kept for him. I wrote down how much he weighed, and when he learned to walk, things like that. There is a lock of his hair from his first haircut, and a few pictures. I just thought you would like to have it."

Ginny was teary eyed, "You were right about that. I will want to do that, too. That's just the sweetest thing to have, thank you."

"This is a blanket that he was wrapped in when he was baptized. And this is the rattle that his Armbruster grandparents bought him when he was born. Just little keepsakes."

Ginny hugged Mom and kissed her on the cheek. "This is about the nicest gift I've ever gotten. So much tradition for our baby to share."

"Yes, Mom, I didn't even know you had these things"

"Well, there hadn't been an occasion to give them to you until now."

"Thank you, Mom."

"Now, I want a proper look around. Show me everything, I want to see what you have done."

They started in the living room since they were already there. She admired the television set and thought that the outlets in the floor were very clever. She loved the new bedroom suite and the dining room furniture. "I notice you don't have much to fill that China cabinet."

Now we just have the dishes we use every day and it's not really convenient to keep them in here.

"Hmmm, I see. Well, lead on. Show me what you have done outside."

They started by the pool. They had cleaned the patio area around the pool and added some large pots for plants. They didn't have patio furniture yet, just a few folding chairs.

"Show me that garage you told me about, with the little apartment."

"The apartment is rough, Mom. It's more like it used to be an apartment."

"Well, let's see."

She looked through the apartment carefully. They had cleaned all the trash out so you could walk through just fine, but it was still a mess. "This door opens to the garage?"

"Yes ma'am, I have a key for that right here." Danny opened it so they could walk from the apartment into the garage. The garage was just one open room with windows on either side and two large doors that opened out like barn doors. The walls were unfinished on the inside but the building itself looked quite sturdy.

The apartment itself was just one long room, with a small living area and a galley kitchen. The bathroom was just shower, sink and toilet, no bathtub, but the fixtures weren't bad. The kitchen had a good double sink and cabinets but would need a stove and refrigerator to really be a kitchen again. The linoleum was worn and cracked, and the walls begged for a coat of paint. Mom looked things over and said she was ready to go back and take a better look at the snack tray that Ginny had put out.

They settled into the living room and Mom said, "I had an idea that I wanted to talk to you about. Danny, do you think that garage building is structurally sound?"

"Yes Mom, it was inspected before we bought the house."

"That's good, that's good. And how is the plumbing. Is it all intact?"

"Yes, the water just needs turned back on."

"Well, here is my thought. I think that the little apartment could be turned into a nice kitchen and breakfast nook. The garage area itself could be a decent living room and bedroom. The door that is there now between apartment and garage could be widened into an archway. The garage doors would even be a nice way to open from the bedroom to a little patio. What do you think?"

"That sounds lovely, Mom and I really hadn't considered expanding it into the garage. That's a very good idea. But we can't spend that kind of money right now. I was just thinking clean and paint the studio and put in the stove and fridge. That is if we decide to hire someone. We haven't really figured it out."

"Well, you have only heard half of my idea. The other part is that I move in there."

"What? Mom? What are you talking about?"

"Only if you want me, but I could be the live-in babysitter. I work cheap and I already love the baby."

Ginny jumped into the conversation, "Mom, that would solve a lot of problems, but what about your house. And would you really want to move all the way out here? You have your friends in Bakersfield."

Danny was nodding along, "Mom, we would love it, but I don't see how it's possible for you. And we can't afford to totally remodel the garage."

"Kids, listen. First of all, if you don't want your mom messing in your life, then the conversation is over and there are no hard feelings. If I'm being honest, having my mother-in-law living within thirty miles would have made me crazy, no offence to your granny dear, so I would understand if it's not a good fit for you."

Ginny and Danny spoke together, "That's not it, we would love to have you here! They looked at each other and smiled.

"Ok, if that's the case, the rest is easy. I sell, my house, have the garage built to suit me and I move in before the baby arrives."

"But Mom, what about your friends and the ladies' clubs and your house? Mom, would you really give up the house?"

"Listen honey. I have some friends in town, but they have families, too. Any real friends will stay in touch. The clubs are just a way to stay busy. The house. I have spent a lot of years there, but you kids don't want it. You want to live out of town, and you have a nice place here. So, it's going to get sold someday, it might as well be while I can enjoy the money. Truth be told, the house is too big for me and it's a lot of work keeping it clean and keeping the yard looking nice. I don't want to complain, but I've been lonely. While you were gone and Ginny helped me with the garden, I had that to look forward to. Then you were home for a while, and it was wonderful. I find things to keep me busy but nothing that would keep me from wanting to be with my grandchild."

"Aw Mom, I didn't know you felt that way. I thought you were living it up now that you have the free time."

"Free time and too much time on your hands are close relatives. I'm not complaining, I'm just trying to be honest. There is nothing keeping me in Bakersfield. I can still drive in to church on Sundays and if I wanted to stay involved in a club, I could. You drive it every day, after all."

"Well Mom, It's a generous offer."

"Not at all, Danny. I'm just family. Raising a child is hard. It's a lot easier if you have help."

"Do you even think your house would sell that fast? Sometimes houses are on the market for months."

"I've had offers." Apparently, my property is sought after. Realtors call me from time to time."

"You have all the answers don't you." Danny grinned at his mother.

"I do. Except for one. It's really all up to you and Ginny."

Ginny and Danny looked at each other and had one of those conversations that married couples can have without ever saying a word. They nodded at each other and turned to Mom. Speaking in unison again, the said, "Let's do it."

Mom clapped her hands and squealed. "I'm delighted. Let's get to work then, we have a lot to do and a very short time to do it."

They planned for Mrs. Armbruster to call a realtor on Monday. She knew one that had shown interest before. Danny was going to call a contractor that Ted had recommended for any work they might want done. This was a bigger job than Danny felt comfortable doing himself, especially with the short time to do it. Ted would help them get appliances and take a look at Mrs. Armbruster's furniture to tell her what it was worth. He could buy it from her or sell it on consignment in his store.

They were all so excited that they talked all though dinner and stayed at the table talking after they were all done eating. It was getting late so Mom stayed the night in the guest room rather than driving back to the city after dark.

On Monday, Ginny dropped Danny at the shop and drove to her office. She was settling in at her desk and thinking about how much longer she would be able to work, how she would tell her boss, what his reaction would be...and she just decided that she couldn't take weeks of wondering. She felt somewhat dishonest, and Danny had made a good point; either they valued her as an employee and would work with her or they wouldn't, and she would work somewhere else. She decided it would be better to know, either way.

She knocked on the boss's door and heard him say come in.

"I wondered if I might speak with you for a moment, sir."

"Certainly, Ginny, what can I do for you?"

"Well, sir, I have an announcement to make and I'm not sure how it will affect my position here."

"Sounds serious. Go on."

"Danny and I are expecting a baby. I just found out last week."

"Well, that's wonderful news Ginny! Congratulations! Give Danny my congratulations as well. Now, how will this affect your job. Not leaving us, I hope?"

"Well, no sir, not if you don't want me to."

"Oh, I certainly wouldn't want to lose you Ginny! My wife and I have four children, as you know, so I am aware that there might come a time that you need to slow down a little, but if your doctor says you can work, you can as far as I am concerned. Is Danny ok with you working?"

"Yes, Danny is fine as long as the doctor approves. And the doctor has said that barring unforeseen circumstances I can work until near the end and that will likely be in July."

"You will need time off after the baby comes, of course, but that shouldn't be a problem. You have worked here five years and if I remember correctly have only taken two weeks off in that time, is that right?"

"Yes, sir, it is."

"Then I am sure we can work something out. I'll talk to the partners about hiring someone on a temporary basis while you are away. I may need you to train a girl before you leave, but we have time to think about that."

"Thank you so much sir, I am relieved."

"Ginny, I don't think you know how much we appreciate you're here. You have caught mistakes and helped make corrections that could have cost the firm had you not been here. It has not gone unnoticed by me or the other partners. You're the best secretary I've ever had and if I was foolish enough to let you go, one of the other partners would snap you up!"

"Thank you, sir. I just try to do my job, that's all."

"You do it very well, now, is there anything else I can do for you?"

"No sir, thank you."

"You're welcome, Ginny. I don't forget to tell Danny that I said congratulations. I'm very happy for you both."

Ginny went back to her desk feeling relieved and pleased that she had taken the chance to talk to her boss. That was one less thing to worry about.

As soon as Danny got in the car, Ginny burst out, "My boss says congratulations!"

It took Danny a moment to catch up. "Congratulations about wha...You told him!"

"I did! I couldn't stand not knowing if I would still have a job or not."

"I take it that it went well."

"Very well, I'm almost embarrassed by the praise. I can work as long as I want to and will have a job when I am ready to come back.

I will train a temp to do my work while I'm gone so I won't have to catch up too much when I go back."

"That's very good news. I'm glad you talked to him. I had a feeling it would work out; they love you there."

"I guess they really do."

"I called the contractor today. He said he could come look at the garage anytime this week. I called Ted and he said he could meet him there tomorrow and show him the space and tell him what we are thinking. That way we don't have to wait until Saturday to get him started."

"That's good. Does Ted know what we want?"

"I gave him a rough idea and he has a pretty good idea of what we like. But we will meet with the contractor on Saturday to go over everything and can make changes then."

"He will probably want money to get started."

"He probably will. We can move things around if we have to, and we can call Mom when we get home and see how she did with the realtor."

When they walked through the door the phone was ringing. Danny dashed over to answer it. "Hello." He waved Ginny over. "It's Mom."

They held the phone between them so they could both hear. "Ok, Mom. We are both here. What did you find out?"

"Didn't I tell you my house was sought after? I called the realtor, and he is coming tomorrow with *two* interested buyers. He said if I am ready to sell, we could have a contract by the end of the week."

"Mom that is amazing. I love our house, but why is it so popular I wonder?"

"Families honey. So many young people are starting families since the war ended. This four-bedroom house looks pretty good to people with growing families. There is a new elementary school just a block away and the park is adding playground equipment. This big old house in a family neighborhood with just one old lady living in it is a waste!"

"I don't think you are over-the-hill yet, Mom."

"Oh, you know what I mean. This house is for young people. Since it's not likely you will want it, this is the best plan."

"Just make sure you get a fair price. Don't rush to sell if the price isn't right."

"Honey, the realtor works on commission. I think he is going to try for a good price."

Danny filled his mother in on the progress he had made with the contractor and gave the phone to Ginny so she could tell her how her day went.

When Ginny got hung up the phone, the house smelled wonderful, and she went to the kitchen to find that Danny had their dinner well underway. She had prepared a meatloaf yesterday and left it in the refrigerator. Danny had it in the oven and was boiling potatoes to mash and had a can of corn ready to heat on the stove. He was busy cutting fruit into a bowl for their dessert.

"Danny I was going to do all this."

"I know, and your prep work yesterday made it easy. Thank you for making an easy menu to follow. I told you to get used to being pampered. You are carrying the heir, that's your job."

"The heir, huh?"

"Yes, the heir to *all* of this." He waved his arm.

"Oh my. Such importance. But quit being silly, I can cook."

"No ma'am. If you are going to continue working a full-time job, you are going to let me fill in where I can. Now go put your feet up. I have spoken!"

She laughed as she headed back to the living room. "I will, but I worry about your delusions of grandeur."

In mid-January Ginny called her mother to tell her the news. She was three months pregnant, and Doctor Johnson had said she was in perfect health. Her mother seemed truly delighted that she and Greta were both going to give her grandchildren this year.

She hung up the phone and turned to Danny with wide eyes. "She offered to come stay when the baby is born."

"She *what*?" Danny looked as horrified as she felt. He quickly re-covered. "So, um, what did you say?"

"Don't worry, I talked her out of it. I told her Greta would need her."

"Oh, poor Greta." He clapped his hand over his mouth. So much for trying to stay neutral.

"My thoughts exactly, you don't have to pretend with me dear. I know very well what a trial my mother can be."

"She has her good points."

"She does. But she would drive us crazy if she were here."

"I have to agree."

It was only about three weeks later that Ginny got a call from her mother that JT had passed away.

## 22

# The Cottage

Ginny was gobsmacked. She couldn't say she had ever loved JT, but he had been her stepfather for a long time and she was sure she was supposed to feel something. All she could come up with though was surprised. She had just assumed he would recover and make everyone's life difficult for years to come.

She couldn't imagine her mother without JT but considering how she had taken over the farm in the wake of his stroke, she had a feeling she would be all right.

But it made her think about how fast life could change. She and Greta were both expecting. She and Danny had their "mini farm" and were adding a cottage for Mom to live in. Chet and Greta were building on to their house, too. And now JT was gone. So much had changed just since they had visited Arkansas last spring.

Mother had been thoughtful on the phone. Ginny was sure she would want her to drop everything to come for the funeral, but Mother had been more concerned for her welfare.

They never discussed Mother and JT's stillborn child. Mother had gotten pregnant soon after they moved to Arkansas. It would probably have been considered a "change of life" baby; Mother had been over forty. Ginny hadn't been there, of course, but she had received

153

letters from Mother and Chet saying that the baby didn't live. All she knew was that it was a little girl, and she was buried in Starkville.

But as an expectant mother herself now, she couldn't imagine the thought of losing a baby. The very idea made her shiver and hold her belly as if she could protect her baby better by holding on. She had never thought of how horrible it must have been or how Mother must have mourned.

So, her fearing for Ginny and her baby made sense. She wouldn't want to take any chances.

Danny asked her if she felt like they should make the trip anyway, just to spend time with her family. Ginny said that she thought it would be more upsetting to her mother if they did. She didn't want to worry her.

After the funeral she got a letter from Greta telling her that JT had bought US Savings Bonds for Alton. She said how surprised they had all been that Mother hadn't even known. Ginny snorted at that part. He probably used Mother's money. Then she chastised herself for thinking ill of the dead. He had done a nice thing.

Greta said that Mother was going to start savings for both of their babies and buy bonds for them as soon as they had names to put on the bonds.

"Danny come read this." She pointed to the paragraph about the savings bonds.

"Well, isn't that a surprise? And very nice of your mother to make arrangements for the babies."

"I guess you were right about the 'heir' after all. There will be an inheritance!"

"Even better. They can get this when the bonds mature."

"Very good point. No need to give them incentive to get rid of us!"

The remodel on the garage was making progress. Mom had used some savings to get the contractor started but the house was under contract, and she would have money soon. She had indeed, gotten a good price for the house, more than Danny had expected her to get.

They needed the house to sell to pay for the remodel but it left Mom without a home until the cottage was completed.

"You will move into the guest room, that's easy," was Danny's response.

"Now Son, don't you think you will be wanting to make a nursery in there?"

"That's true but we have time for that. Ginny wants the baby to sleep in our room for the first few months. We don't have much to do in there but change the furniture. The room was just painted. It's no trouble at all."

So that was settled easily but then came the actual move. Mom had thirty days to clear out the house of thirty years of accumulation. As often happened, Ted came to the rescue. He looked over all of Mom's furniture and helped her pick out the pieces that she would want in her cottage. Then he made an inventory of all the things that were to be sold and made her an offer to buy them outright. It would take months to sell things on consignment and he made her a very generous offer, so she took him up on it.

There was one piece of furniture that Ted took to his shop to restore for her, and it was their little secret. I was the cradle that her grandfather had made for her, and she had used it for Danny. The wood had darkened over the years and there were a few scratches, so he took it to sand and seal the wood. He did an excellent job, Mrs. Armbruster didn't think it had ever looked so good! They saved it as a little surprise for Danny and Ginny.

The furniture was the biggest part of the move, but the real work came in sorting everything else. Room by room she needed to sort things to move, things to donate to charity and things to burn. There was just so much! Ginny and Danny helped but, in the end, she had to hire two young ladies from her church who could just carry things out for her. A great pile was made to be donated to the church for the annual rummage sale. Fortunately, the church sent a truck for that. When she had narrowed it down to things she wanted to keep, there was one more issue to overcome, where to put it all until the cottage was ready. Ted came to the rescue again. He roped of a section of his warehouse to store everything and when the time came his employees would bring it all to the cottage.

Ginny continued to work even as she got bigger and bigger. She was one of those women that thrived on being pregnant. Once she got passed the morning sickness, which had never been terrible, she felt healthier than she ever had.

When she heard that Greta was confined to her bed, she felt horrible for her. She couldn't even imagine how crazy she would go if she had to stay in bed. She sent her cards and books to read to try to help with the boredom.

As the cottage began to take shape Ginny, was impressed with how her mother-in-law's vision was coming to life. The old barn-style doors were reenforced and insulated and were bolted so that you could choose to open both or just one. The old driveway became a beautiful patio, and with the doors opened it was like having the bedroom outside. There were screen doors that slid into wall pockets so she could enjoy the breeze without the pests.

New countertops and cabinets went into the bathroom and kitchen areas and modern appliances gave the old galley kitchen a very modern look. She had considered a washing machine, but Ginny and Danny had purchased one, with baby laundry, Ginny felt it would be a necessity, so she could easily wash her clothes in their house.

It was going to be beautiful, and the truly remarkable thing was, it looked like it would be finished before the baby's arrival!

# 23

## Greta's Surprise

Greta couldn't have been more disappointed. She stayed in bed all week except to go the bathroom and to take a quick wash at the kitchen sink. Chet helped her change from a night gown into a dress every morning, so she at least felt like a person. She couldn't stand the thought of laying around in her nightgown all day.

So, when Doctor Jeffries said he wanted her in bed another week, she almost cried. Well, she did cry but not until he was gone.

He had brought a scale with him, and he weighed her and measured her belly. She didn't seem to be bleeding anymore and that was a good sign.

He asked Chet to come join them when he was done examining Greta.

"Greta, you still haven't gained any weight. Are you eating?"

"Yes, Doc. I eat."

"She doesn't eat everything I put on her plate," Chet chimed in.

"Tattletale! And you pile a plate like I'm a field hand!"

Doctor Jeffries looked at her sternly. "Greta you truly are eating for two. That's not just a saying. If you can't finish a plate at mealtime, I want you to snack in between meals. I want you drinking water, you are still a little dehydrated and that can be very dangerous for the baby. I also want you to drink milk, and juice. Your herbal tea is good but no black tea or coffee for a while. I want you eating beef, and cheese and cottage cheese and fruits. Bananas are a good snack. You should have a drink beside you at all times and if you had some snacks nearby, so you don't need to ask. Apples, bananas, crackers."

Chet took it all in. "We can do that. I'll keep food here for her."

"Try to find things to tempt her. We need weight on this girl. And drink!"

He left and tears of frustration poured down Greta's cheeks. "I want to follow doctor's orders, and I'll do what I have to for a healthy baby, but I am bored to tears. Really and truly bored to tears."

"I know you are. I'll be right back." Chet went and got her a tall glass of ice water and set it on the nightstand. On the card table he set down a plate with a package of graham crackers and an apple.

While Mrs. Fleming still has Alton I'm going to run into the grocery store.

Chet went to Starkville, but he didn't go straight to the grocery store. He went to the OTASCO store and made a beeline for the television sets. The clerk came over to help him, but Chet knew what he had in mind. He picked out a portable set. It had a thirteen-inch screen and Chet though it would sit just fine on the old Victrola case that Greta had brought home from her folk's house. He could put it on the wall at the end of their bed, and she could watch TV to pass the time.

He was looking at antennas and the clerk helped him work out what was needed. "Mr. Masters, where you folks live down in the valley, the rabbit ears aren't going to get you any reception. You will need an outside antenna and a tall one. This is the one I would recommend. It's pretty powerful. The closest station is in Tulsa, so you need a good antenna, up high and aimed at Tulsa."

He and Chet figured how much wire he would need, and he had some pipe that would work for a pole. He needed one more thing before he completed his purchase.

"Could I borrow your phone?"

He dialled the Reddington's number and Greta's Ma answered. He explained to her what the doctor had said, and he asked if Bill would be free to help him with a project.

"I'm sending him right over and I'll send some provisions with him, too."

Chet hung up the phone and asked the clerk if he had a check book for the bank in Grove, where his account was. It had added up to a fair amount and he didn't have that much cash with him.

"I do have a check book for that bank, but Mr. Masters, you don't have to pay it all today. With a small down payment, I could spread payments out over the next year. Pay once a month. There is a small fee up front but if you pay on time it won't cost you anymore."

He pulled out a book with the payment schedule and fee for the amount he was paying and it all looked real fair to him, so he said, "Let's do it!" He paid cash for the down payment and walked out with everything he needed to get Greta a TV installed.

He made his stop at the grocery store to pick up some fruit and cookies that he knew Greta liked. Alton would be happy about the cookies, too.

Bill was pulling in the driveway the same time Chet did. He got out and asked what the big project was.

Chet shushed him and pointed in the window to the truck seat. The TV was sitting there in all its glory.

"I'll be! For Greta? I'll be stuck in bed if I get a TV."

"Keep your trap shut, it's a surprise. We have to get some of those pipes welded together and I figure mount to this side of the house for the antenna. We need to work quick."

"Ok, well Ma sent over about all the food in the house, I'm not sure what she kept for us to eat, so I'll carry that in."

"Yeah, I bought a few things, too."

Bill carried in a gallon of fresh milk, some butter and a huge crock of cottage cheese. He had an armload of beets and turnips and taters that Ma had brought out of the root cellar. She said there was nothing like root vegetables to get your blood running again. Whatever that meant.

Greta was surprised to see Bill. "Oh, I called your Ma to see if she had fresh milk. She sent Bill over. Since he's here, he's gonna help me with a project.

"What project?"

Bill chimed in, "Why, working on your castle, your Majesty."

"Thank you, peasant, but speak only when spoken to."

"Oh, forgive me. I will away, lest I displease you again."

"Character." Greta said as he went out the door.

Chet showed her the cookies he got for her, and he was happy to see her reach for a couple. He left the package on her table.

She said, "Alton likes these, too. When will he be back, I'm bored without him."

"I'm sure Mrs. Fleming will have him back by supper, but Greta you aren't going to be chasing him around."

"I know. I just miss him is all.

"I know you do. Hey, I need to work while I've got Bill here. I'll check on you in a little while."

"Ok. I'll read another darned book!"

Chet went out to find Bill. He had already started fitting pipe together. "How tall do you think we need to go?"

As tall as we can but we need to be able to reach the antenna if I need to so only six feet taller than the peak of the roof, I guess.

In the end they put their heads together and made a tripod that they could bolt right to the roof. The made a bracket with nuts that would tighten down to hold the pipe in place or could be loosened to drop the antenna lower if it needed adjustment. By doing it that way, they managed to get ten feet above the roof, not six.

Chet and Bill carried it all up on the roof and bolted it down. Chet attached the wires to the antenna and tied the wire to the pole so it would stay secure. Then he dropped the rest to the ground. It was time to hook it up.

"How are you going to run it inside?"

"I'll drill a hole and fix it right tomorrow but for tonight I'm running it in the window. Now aim that thing at Tulsa and let's get off the roof."

Chet went in to check on Greta. "What in the world were you doing on the roof?"

"Man stuff, don't worry your pretty little head about it."

"Chet..."

"Just give me a minute, you'll see." He went to the window and grabbed the wire Bill was feeding into him. He pulled a good length of it in, and Bill ran around to the front porch. He wanted to be there to see Greta's face, too.

Chet reached out and grabbed the Television and turned around where Greta could see it. Bill was peaking over his shoulder to watch Greta. It was worth it.

At first, she couldn't quite figure out what he was holding. She had seen televisions at the store and in pictures in the magazines, but she hadn't thought she would see one in her house anytime soon. When realization dawned, she was struck dumb. She looked from Chet to Bill and back to Chet. Her mouth moved but no words came out.

Bill said, "I think she's surprised."

Chet answered, "I think she is."

"Oh, my lord Chet, where did that come from?"

"Otasco."

"I mean what is it doing here?"

"I bought it for you."

"You never did!"

"Yes, I did."

"For me?"

"All for you. The only time I will touch it is if you tell me to change the channel."

"But why?"

"Well, I thought you would figure that part out. I can't have you bored to actual tears, now, can I?"

"Oh Chet, I'm a big ol' cry-baby. I don't deserve a TV."

"Yes, you do, and I already bought it and it's done. Now let me set it down, it's heavy."

"Where you puttin' it?"

"On your old Victrola case and then right at the end of the bed so you can see it. And I'm thinking now that I should have moved the case before I brought this in. Bill would you out that case over by that wall, right in front of Greta?"

Bill moved quick and Chet was able to put the set down. It was just like he thought, it fit just right.

"That won't fall on Alton, will it?"

"No. Its sturdy. I will keep the wires where he can't reach."

"It only took a few minutes to get the antenna wire hooked up then he plugged it in and turned it on.

After a few minutes it came on, with nothing but a white screen that looked like a snowstorm.

Give me just a minute to try the channels. He turned the dial slowly to see if a picture appeared. The clerk had told him that there were three Tulsa stations, but he might not get them all. From what he could see, they got the ABC network crystal clear. NBC was fair and CBS you could hear but barely see.

Greta was doing her best not to bounce up and down, but she was so excited she feltlike she was going to lift off the bed!

"I don't care if its one channel! I'll watch what is on it! Just get out of the way!"

Chet laughed and tuned it back to the ABC station.

Greta was true to her word. She had no idea what program was on, but she was glued to it!

That was the scene when Mother and Mrs. Fleming walked in. When Mother arrived home from school she was greeted by Alton, and she said she would just walk with him and Mrs. Fleming to bring him home and check to see what the Doctor had said.

She and Mrs. Fleming were both about as surprised as Greta had been. Alton however was just interested to see what was going on. He crawled up in his spot beside Greta and just started watching along with her.

Chet smiled and took his mother and Mrs. Fleming into the kitchen to fill them in on what the doctor had said.

"So, I went to Otasco and bought the TV. I know it's a big expense, but she was going crazy. She's not going to stay in that bed if she is bored out of her mind."

"No, you did right, I think." Mother said. I would have done it, too. Did you have the money to spend?"

"I did but just barely. I was going to write a check, but the clerk told me I could make payments. It was just a small fee as long as I pay it on time. If I'm late it's another story, but I won't be late."

"No. I'm sure you won't. You are doing a good job taking care of your family." Chet beamed at the praise.

The next day, on her lunch break from school, Mrs. Smith walked into the Otasco and paid off the TV in full.

# 24

# Time Off

Ginny continued to feel perfectly healthy but by the end of her seventh month she was starting to have some swelling in her feet by the end of the day and was getting fatigued more easily. In June, her doctor recommended that she work half days if possible. She suggested that to her boss and again, he was surprisingly supportive.

"Ginny, I think that's a great idea. Next week let's get that temp in here and you can start training her. You can work the mornings and leave at noon. Then we can see how she does on her own before you actually take time off. Yes, I think that's a fine idea."

"Thank you, sir. I'll call the College and see if they have a likely candidate."

As it turned out, the college had just the girl for them. She needed one semester to graduate but working as an intern over the summer would help offset some credits she needed. The stipend that the firm would pay for her expenses was very little, compared to Ginny's salary. The girl, Stephanie, would be available to intern until classes started in September. The timing was perfect!

That evening Ginny told Danny all about it on the way home. He was glad to here that she was going to be working shorter days.

"But it does mean we have a transportation issue, if I'm not going to pick you up in the evenings."

"That's not a big problem. Either I will drive Mom's Buick, or you or Mom can pick me up in the evenings. We can play it by ear."

The following week, Stephanie arrived for her first day and Ginny gave her a quick tour and started her training right away. She hovered over her at first, checking her shorthand, proofreading her typing, but was soon satisfied that she knew what she was doing. She was nervous to leave her at noon on her first day, but everyone assured her that they business wouldn't collapse if she were gone for the day.

She drove home and went into an empty house. Mom was out by the cottage planting some flowers she had brought from her old house. So, for the moment Ginny was alone in the house. It felt strange. Not that she had never been alone in the house, but she always came home from work with Danny. She really didn't know what to do now that she was home.

She turned on the TV to warm it up, then went to make a sandwich for her lunch.

She sat down in front of the television as Mom came in. "I thought I heard you come in. I see you found yourself some lunch."

"I did. I don't really know how to be a lady of leisure, though."

"You're doing fine so far!"

"Yes, there is some surprisingly good programming in the daytime. I may turn into a television addict. I can see how it has been a blessing for Greta" Greta had written her that Chet brought in a television as a surprise for her on her second week of bed rest. And thank heavens he had. She had spent the rest of her pregnancy in bed or when Doctor Jeffries finally approved it, sitting on the sofa. Even since giving birth three weeks ago she was on partial bed rest. Ginny would have lost her mind.

"Oh, I doubt it, dear. You are far to active to sit still for too long."

"And I suppose there is a baby to prepare for. We haven't done much yet."

"I have good news on that front! I'm moving into the cottage next week!"

"Next week? They are going to finish *ahead* of schedule? Unheard of!"

"I think Ted has been bullying them a little, "Mom laughed. "He has certainly kept them motivated."

"So have you asked Ted when he can have your furniture here?"

"He says next Tuesday, as long as he gets the final 'all clear' from the contactor. If all goes as planned, I expect I will spend Wednesday night in my new home."

"That is wonderful! Well, shopping for baby furniture and a layette are definitely on my list now!"

"You are supposed to be off work to rest, let's not plan too much."

"Oh, it will be fun. We can go shopping together and I can rest if I get tired. Danny will want to look at furniture, too, so we can go this Saturday maybe."

Mom made a quick trip to her room and came back with an armful of magazines.

"Here honey, get started." She handed Ginny a pile of catalogs, and two recent issues of 'Baby Talk' magazine. She also handed her a pad of paper and a pencil. The TV was soon forgotten as Ginny became absorbed making notes of what would be needed. When Mom came back through to check on her she had curled up on the couch and was asleep, note pad still in hand. Mom covered her with a throw and turned off the television.

# 25

## Arrival

Thank the Lord for television! Doctor Jeffries continued to recommend bedrest for Greta, and she was really starting to hate it. By the middle of March, he said he felt a little more comfortable with her moving around the house some, but no standing for long periods, no lifting and she could go outside for some fresh air if Chet was with her, and she didn't over exert herself. So at least she could spend part of the day on the sofa instead of in bed. Chet would turn the TV for her so she could see it.

Doctor Jeffries continued to make house calls to see her. He didn't want her coming into town in Chet's old truck over that bumpy road. He told her the other choice was to put her in the hospital in Grove for the duration of her pregnancy, so she suddenly appreciated the freedoms that she had at home. There would be no TV or snuggles from Alton if she was in the hospital.

Chet and Bill had finished the addition to the house and Greta thought having a flush toilet in the house was the lap of luxury. The water heater wasn't hooked up right away but even having cold water to the sink and tub was nice. Chet could boil water for her to heat bathwater, and she could actually sit in a warm bath. He planned to have the water heater connected before much longer.

Greta and Chet didn't move into the new bedroom right away. Greta wanted to stay in the living room where she could see the TV and she could watch Alton play in his room from her bed. Chet put their Chest of drawers in the bedroom and that made more room in the living room for now. That was nice.

Doctor Jeffries talked to Chet about a plan for the birth. He thought it would be best to move Greta to the hospital about a week before her due date so she would be there for the birth in case there were complications. "You know I have had serious concerns for Greta and the baby. Her delivery might go just fine, it probably will, but just in case, I would rather have her in the hospital in case something does go wrong."

"Ok, then that's what we will do."

"She is due near the end of May, we will get her in the last week of May to be on the safe side"

But at usual Greta had plans of her own. Two weeks before her due date she felt labor pains starting. She got up and went to the phone to call Doctor Jeffries and her water broke. She made the call and Doctor Jeffries said, "Get back in bed and wait for me. I will be right there. Try to relax."

Greta did one more thing before she went back to the bed. She went to the front door and reached out to ring the big dinner bell.

Chet heard the bell and came running as fast as he could. Alton was with Mrs. Fleming at Mother's house and Greta was alone. He ran through the front door and found her hunched over the bed in pain. Her dress and the floor were wet.

"Greta what is it?"

"I'm in labor Chet. I already called Doctor Jeffries, he is coming as fast as he can. I need you to do a few things."

"Whatever you need."

"I need you to get towels. Bring them all. Go get me a clean night gown. Hurry"

He ran as fast as he could and gathered what she needed.

"Ok, help me out of this wet dress." He unzipped the dress and pulled it over her head. He dropped it on the floor and helped her into her nightdress. She pulled the gown hallway down and dropped her panties to the floor.

"Ok. Spread two or three towels on the bed, midway down." As soon as that was done, she gratefully crawled in the bed. Another contraction hit as she lay back on the pillows. She grimaced in pain. They were coming fast and hard. She was very relieved to hear Doctor Jeffries car zooming up the driveway. He slammed the car door and came running into the house, carrying his bag.

"Ok, Greta. Tell me what is going on."

"Well since I talked to you, I have had three contractions. The last one was hard!"

"Ok. I'm going to check your really quick to see how advanced you are." He did a pelvic exam and looked at Greta with surprise. "How long were you having contractions before you called me Greta?"

"I had one that I wasn't sure was a contractions at first. My back just sort of ached and I rolled on my side. A few minutes later I had one and when I got up to call you my water broke."

"Ok, well Greta, we are about to greet this baby. When you feel the next contraction start pushing."

Chet said, "What can I do."

"Chet, I forgot you were here. What you can to is hold Greta's hand. Wait. Do you have warm water?"

"I got the water heater installed a couple of days ago, so yes we do."

"That's just fine then. Just hold Greta's hand for now. Greta are you ready? Push!"

She pushed until the contraction eased off. Doctor Jeffries told her to take a minute to breathe, but she didn't have long before the next contraction hit.

"This baby is ready to be here! Your doing fine Greta. Take a quick breath and give me one more hard push."

Greta pushed with all her might and then felt a rush of relief. In the next second she and Chet heard a small cry. Their baby was here!"

Doctor Jeffries examined the baby carefully and wrapped it in a towel. "Chet I could use some warm water now. Make sure the basin is clean."

Chet brought water back in a hurry. He heard Greta say, "What do we have Doctor a boy or a girl? Is it ok?"

"You have a little girl and right now she is struggling a little bit to get her breath," He swept he mouth with a bulb syringe and cleared some mucous. Chet and Greta heard the baby's cry again, this time much stronger. "There we go. Much better."

He dipped the end of a towel in the water and carefully wiped the baby's face. He wrapped her tight in a clean towel and handed her to Greta. "Meet your daughter. She was certainly anxious to meet you."

After that Doctor Jeffries wrapped up the soiled towels and took them away to the and helped Chet get a couple of dry towels under her. The baby had ceased her cries and was now looking at Greta as if studying her.

"I don't believe that baby was early at all. We must have miscalculated the dates. She is perfectly healthy. Greta, you called me thirty-five minutes before this young lady appeared. I barely made it in time. I've never seen a labor progress so fast."

"My back was achy all day yesterday, but nothing that felt like labor."

"Well, you are a marvel, young lady. Your baby is healthy, and you seem fine. I still want you in bed for a while, don't go jumping up Just yet."

"Oh, I don't feel like jumping just now."

"Are you planning to breast feed?"

"You know Doctor, after the trouble with Alton and as hard of a time as I had gaining weight, I don't think I want to try this time. I think I would just rather her start on formula."

"I think it's wise. She probably won't take more than half ounce at a time for the first day or two but feed her as often as she wants. I don't hold with this scheduling idea for feeding. I think babies know when they are hungry."

"I think so, too."

"Well, I'll be going now. Call if you feel like anything is off. And Chet, I bet you have some calls to make."

Greta looked wide-eyed. "Oh, my Lord, Chet! Nobody knows. Everyone thinks I've got two weeks, to go!"

"Yeah, I reckon I do have some calls to make."

~~~

After Chet had called Greta's folks he called Mrs. Fleming. She would inform mother as soon as she got home from school. She said they would come over after that and bring Alton. For now, it was just Chet and Greta and their daughter. Chet had started formula and was sitting by Greta, admiring the baby

"Everyone is going to want to know her name." Chet whispered over his sleeping daughters head.

"Then we better decide on one."

"Both of my grandmothers were named Louise. Maybe that for a middle name."

"That's fine. What do you want to call her?"

"Do you like the name 'Clara'?"

"I like it. Clara Louise?"

"I think so."

"Well, hello, Clara."

When Mother and Mrs. Fleming brought Alton in, they showed him the baby and said her name was Clara.

"Cara", he repeated.

Greta looked at Chet, "I think I like that better."

Chet laughed and said, Ginny named me, I guess Alton named Cara."

"Cara it is."
~~~

Alton smiled, "Cara!"

# 26

# Another Arrival

After Ginny heard about Greta's home delivery, she had high hopes. A thirty-minute labor sounded fine to her! But Doctor Johnson told her not to get her hopes up, first babies have a way of taking their time.

She and Mom had picked out baby clothes and lightweight blankets for a July baby. Danny had helped her pick out a crib and changing table. They repainted the chest of drawers from the guest room to match the new furniture and it looked nice together.

All of the new clothes, diapers and blankets had been washed and put away. As a working mother, Ginny planned to bottle feed from the start. They bought a sterilizer, bottles and one of the new pre-mixed formula's.

Everything was ready.

After working half days for about three weeks, Ginny felt like Stephanie had everything under control, so she went ahead and started her maternity leave. She only had a couple of weeks until her due date.

Her boss had talked to the other partners, and they decided that since she had only taken one vacation since she started with them and Stephanie was working through a program with the college and not taking a full wage, that they would offer her half wages for eight weeks. That should allow six weeks after the baby was born, before she needed to come back. She was touched by their generosity.

Danny was thrilled to hear about that. It was definitely acknowledgment of Ginny's value, but also the extra cash would help. Mom had paid for the entire remodel on the Cottage, thank goodness, but with new furniture, washing machine, baby clothes, and doctor visits, the wallet was a little thin. He still had the back up of dipping into the business, but this looked like they wouldn't need to.

So, it was all planned, perfectly. Ginny left work two weeks before the baby was due and everything was ready, so all she had to do was relax. Except Ginny had no experience with relaxing so she wasn't very good at it. TV didn't hold her interest for very long. She read a few books and flipped through baby magazines. Thank goodness it was only a couple of weeks!

Except when the due day came and went and no sign of labor. She saw her doctor the day after her due date and he said, "I told you before Ginny. First babies have their own schedule. Everything looks fine but I don't see any sign that you are going in to labor soon. That could change all at once, but it could be another week."

She saw him the next week. When he told her there was still no change, she didn't know whether to cry or strangle him with his necktie. Danny was in the waiting room, and he could tell from Ginny's stormy expression that she hadn't gotten the answer she was looking for.

"Nothing to do but wait", she said through gritted teeth as they walked to the car.

"Ginny, it's not the doctors fault. The baby will come when it's ready."

"He could get it out of me!"

"You don't mean that. You know the safest thing is to let nature take its course."

"That is so much easier for you to say, than for me to live."

"I know, honey." He did know. Ginny had been in a horrible mood since she took off of work. Now, they were cutting into her time that she was to have with the baby before she went back to work. She was hot, her back ached, her feet swelled; she may have breezed through the first eight months, but this last one was a killer.

His mom told him this was all pretty normal. She had been no pleasure to be around when she was heavily pregnant. And the hottest part of summer was no fun.

The godsend was the pool. It was in partial shade in the afternoon, so Ginny could float on a raft and nap or sit in a chaise by the water reading a magazine and stay cool. She said the only time her back didn't ache was floating in the pool.

After her doctor appointment she went to the pool for a while. Then she went in and refolded all of the diapers and baby clothes and put them away again. She changed the sheets on their bed. She took a shower and washed her hair. She repacked her suitcase for the hospital to make sure everything was there.

Danny thought she might be losing her mind. He had taken the rest of the day off, after her appointment, so he was watching as she went from one bizarre task to another. He went over to the cottage to talk to Mom about it all.

She laughed when he described everything that was going on. "You may want to get a nap in son, you might be in for a busy night."

"What do you mean?"

"She's nesting. And ever efficient, our Ginny is doing it all at once. She will be in labor before you know it. If night tonight, then tomorrow."

"The doctor said she wasn't showing any signs."

"She will be. It goes like that sometimes. Some women start showing signs a week before, some don't until they are in labor. Like I said, Ginny is efficient, why would we expect her to change now?"

When he went back in, Ginny was starting preparations for dinner. He shooed her out of the kitchen. "You know I was planning on doing this. You go put your feet up. You have been running around all afternoon."

"Ok. But don't you think these curtains should be washed?"

"If they need washed, Mom will do it. Go sit. Maybe nap before dinner."

"Oh, I don't think I could nap but maybe I could write a couple of letters. I could write Mother and let her know how stubborn her third grandchild is."

"Yes, you do that."

When he checked on her next, she was sitting in the sofa with her feet up and her small writing desk on her lap. From the stack of envelopes beside her it looked like she had started the Christmas cards early this year, but he didn't ask. He just quietly stepped back into the kitchen.

At dinner, Mom asked Ginny how she had spent her day.

"Oh, the usual. Just sat around staring at the walls." Danny gave his mother a look of surprise and she gave him a quick nod.

Ginny went on. "I did address a lot of envelopes so it we ever have a baby to announce, the envelopes are ready."

Mystery solved.

Mom said, Ginny you should probably try to turn in early tonight. Before long, you will have a little one interrupting your sleep. You might want to catch up while you can."

"I have a little one interrupting my sleep now. But I will try. I will at least lie in bed and read if I can't sleep."

"That would be good."

After watching a bit of TV with Danny and Mom, Ginny made good on her word and went to bed. Mom helped Danny tidy the kitchen and then said, "I'm off to my bed. You get some rest. Call me if there are changes."

I will, Mom.

Danny got ready for bed. Ginny had fallen asleep reading her book, but Danny was afraid to wake her, so he just slipped in bed beside her and left her lamp on. He went right to sleep. Around two a.m. Ginny patted him on the shoulder. "Danny, something is odd."

He was immediately on his feet. "What is it?"

"Well, I feel uncomfortable. Like the baby is scrunching up and then stretching out."

He watched as the baby rolled and changed position. He had seen it move but this was big!

"And Danny, are the sheets damp?"

He felt near her. The sheets were a little damp. She reached for his hand and stood up. Her face registered shock!

"Danny, I..." She pulled her nightdress back to show a trickle of water running down the inside of her thigh.

"Is that the waters breaking? I thought there would be more."

Danny said, "We keep hearing that everyone has different experiences. I'm going to call Doctor Johnson."

"Ok. Maybe you should." Ginny didn't like to make a fuss, but this seemed odd. She had another scrunchy feeling in her belly. She also noticed that for the first time in three weeks her back *didn't* hurt.

"Doctor Johnson will meet us at the hospital. He is calling them now to expect us. He said they would meet us at the front door with a wheelchair. Now, let's put your robe on and I will get my pants and shoes on."

"I would really rather get dressed. This gown is damp."

"Ginny, they will give you a gown at the hospital and you have some in your bag. We need to get you in the car."

"Danny, I'm sure I have time to..."

"Really? Greta didn't."

She put on her robe. Danny pulled on his pants, stuck his feet in some loafers and grabbed a shirt. He picked up Ginny's suitcase. "Are you ready?"

"Yes. I want my purse, and maybe you should take your wallet?"

"Good point. Now are we ready."

"I think so."

He walked her to the car and then got in and started the engine. It was all he could do to drive down the driveway at a normal speed and pull out onto the black top without gunning it. All the way to Bakersfield, he felt like he was going twenty miles per hour, but the speedometer said sixty. The drive had never taken so long. Ginny was serene, not a care in the world.

Well maybe one. She was horribly afraid that this was a false alarm and that she would be embarrassed. She had seen the doctor a few hours ago. She wasn't in pain, the trickle of water had slowed down as soon as they got in the car. (She had made Danny grab a towel though to save the seats.) She would be mortified if she was wasting everyone's time.

At long last (in Dannys opinion) they arrived at the hospital. Danny pulled very close to the door and a nurse appeared with a wheelchair and help Ginny into it. She instructed Danny where to park the car and took Ginny inside.

When Danny came in carrying the suitcase, Ginny's purse and his shirt, (He was still in his undershirt) Ginny was still at the admissions desk. She reached for her purse to get the necessary insurance forms. The nurse was checking her pulse and making notes on a chart while someone else filled out forms.

Doctor Johnson walked in and saw Danny and Ginny. He addressed the nurse and said, "We can do this later. Let's get this young lady to maternity so I can see what is going on."

Danny exhaled and realized he hadn't been breathing. He wasn't sure he had taken a breath since Ginny woke him up.

In a labor room, they got Ginny into a hospital gown and onto a bed. When she stood out of the wheelchair the trickle of water started down her leg again. She was grateful that the bed was covered in an absorbent padding.

When she settled in Doctor Johnson came in and did an exam. "Well, Ginny you are full of surprises. You are about halfway dilated and well on your way. Have you timed your contractions?"

"I didn't know I was having contractions! I've been getting a strange, scrunchy feeling, but it's not painful."

"I'm pretty sure your scrunchy feelings are contractions. Maybe not very strong ones but they seem to be getting the job done. You are leaking fluid. The bag of waters may not be broken, but it is torn enough to let fluid out. I imagine it will go before long. Ginny started having one of those scrunchy feelings again. Doctor Johnson put his hands on her belly to feel it. "Yes, defiantly a contraction. But you don't feel pain?"

"It's uncomfortable, but not bad. Oh, did Danny tell you about the baby moving?"

"He mentioned it, can you describe it?"

"It was like the baby stood up, turned around and took another seat!"

Doctor Johnson laughed, "That's pretty accurate. When I saw you in my office the baby was laying sort of sideways, the head was not at all engaged in your pelvis. Now the head is fully engaged and in the right position for birth. Usually, they do that over a period of days but sometimes it happens all at once.

He looked at Danny who was still holding the suitcase and his shirt.

"Danny you can put that case down. The nurse will show you to the waiting area. Ginny has some work to do here. But we will keep you informed of changes. There is a payphone if you need to make any calls."

"Oh, Mom! I was supposed to call her before we left!"

"I think she will forgive you. But kiss this young lady before you leave, when you see her next, she will be a mother."

Danny gave Ginny a kiss and told her how proud he was of her. She held his hand for a minute but reluctantly let him go. "Now go call your mother and for heavens sake, put your shirt on." He saw that he was still holding the shirt and grinned. He went to call Mom.

The phone rang once before she answered. "I saw your headlights leaving. I told you that you would need a nap!"

"Yes, you did."

"How is she?"

"She is in labor, and the doctor says she is halfway there. She is having contractions, but she can barely feel them."

"Lucky girl. Let's hope it stays that way."

"I'll call you when I know something."

"I'll be right here."

By dawn Danny had read every magazine in the waiting room. He looked at the ashtrays around the room and considered taking up smoking just to have something to do. It must be a slow night, Ginny was the only one in her labor room though there were other beds and Danny had been by himself in the waiting room all night. Nurses had come pretty often to give him reports, and the reports were all the same, "Ginny was doing fine, things are progressing, it could be a while yet."

When the nurse came to give him the same report at six a.m., she suggested he go take a break in the cafeteria. "You can get some breakfast and coffee. If you wanted to, you could even bring a cup of coffee and a doughnut back to the waiting room. But if you want to have breakfast, we can page you if anything happens. It's just down the hall, and to the right."

"Ok, I will do that. You can page me right away if there is any change?"

"We sure can."

"He went to the cafeteria and got himself a tray and filled it with a cup of coffee, a small bowl of fruit, some scrambled eggs and bacon. He paid for his food and sat down at a table right by the door. He started wolfing down food like he had never seen it before, not because he was hungry but because he was listening for his name. He was halfway through his fruit bowl when he heard it. "Danny Armbruster, please return to the maternity ward. Danny Armbruster."

He took a slurp of his coffee and looked around for a place to stow his tray. A waitress waved him on and said, "You go. I'll get that."

He waved his thanks and ran down the hall toward maternity. The same nurse was waiting for him by the waiting area. "She has been taken to the delivery room. She said to tell you she is fine, and she loves you."

"So, everything is ok?"

"Yes, she has been doing very well. I wouldn't expect it to be too much longer. Once they go in the delivery room, things go pretty fast. They will take her back to the labor room when she has delivered. Would you like to wait there for her?"

"Oh yes, please."

He paced the labor room for about twenty minutes before a bed came rolling back into the room with his beautiful wife, positively glowing, and holding a carefully wrapped bundle in her arms.

The put the bed in place and he went and kissed Ginny on the forehead before even daring to peek at the bundle she held. "You did it!"

"I did. Mr. Armbruster, meet your son. She pulled the blanket back a little so that he could see the little pink face of his son.

His son. It all became real to him. What had been a concept was a real person now, right in front of him. He fought back tears.

"What is his name?"

Ginny laughed. "Well, I know we discussed some options, but I thought we would make that final decision together."

"Oh yeah, sure." He was still having trouble grasping that this person was his son.

"Mrs. Armbruster. We have a room ready for you. We need to take baby to the nursery to give him a bath and let the doctor examine him. We will bring him to you when he is ready to have his breakfast."

Ginny reluctantly handed the baby to the nurse.

Mr. Armbruster you can stay for a short visit but then Mrs. Armbruster needs her rest. You may visit this afternoon, between three and five o'clock."

Ginny was thoroughly aggravated. "I think I should get to decide if I'm tired or not. I'm not staying here one minute longer than I have to."

"Good, because I can't wait to get you both home.

~~~

Danny drove home with the plan to take a short nap before returning to the hospital. He had called his mother from the hospital, but she was waiting to hear all the details. He and Ginny had decided to name the baby Wallace Daniel Armbruster. Wallace had been Danny's grandfathers name. They knew he would likely get called Wally, but they decided they could live with it.

Then, after assuring his mom that the baby was beautiful and that she could visit with him later today, he had to call Ginny's mother. He placed the call and Mrs. Fleming answered the phone. When she realized it was Danny on the phone she said, "I'll get Mrs. Smith right away." He heard her say, "It's Danny, he must be calling about Ginny!"

Ginny's mother picked up the phone and asked straight away, "Is she well? Is the baby well?"

"Ginny is doing very well, and our son is very healthy."

"A boy, and he is healthy. Oh, that is just the most wonderful news. When she went past due, I was so concerned."

"We all were, but in the end, everything went very quickly. She woke me at two and the baby was here before seven."

"Then she didn't have a hard time at all. That's good. That's very good. I will pass the information on to Chet and Greta. I won't keep you on the phone longer. Thank you, Danny."

She hung up. Danny though it was a bit abrupt, but Ginny had told him before, when her mother decided a conversation was over, she hung up. If you had something you wanted to say, you better start with it.

He called Ted and let him know the good news.

"Danny Armbruster a father. It's hard to wrap my head around."

"You and me both!"
~~~

"I hope I'm Uncle Ted,"

"Of course you are. Any bad habits he ever learns, we will blame on Uncle Ted."

"I will try to uphold my part of the bargain. I will start thinking up things to teach him right away."

"I believe you."

"So how long will they keep them at the hospital?"

"The usual stay is several days but Ginny was clamouring to come home before I left this morning. I'm not sure they can keep her there."

"Well, let me know. I want to meet my nephew."

Danny did finally get a short nap. His mother woke him so they would have time to drive to the hospital and be there at the beginning of the visiting hours.

They would not let the baby be in the room while they were visiting, but they saw him through the nursery window. As Danny had predicted, Ginny had raised holy hell with Doctor Johnson and he had agreed, reluctantly, to release her the next day, as long as she and the baby had no problems overnight. "They tried to talk me in to staying by saying I could rest here while nurses take care of the baby. I told them Greta had never spent a night in the hospital and she and her babies are fine. The nurse started down a very dangerous path of 'country people' before Doctor Johnson wisely cut her off. So, if there are no problems I will be ready to leave her by noon tomorrow."

"I will be waiting at the nurses station at eleven, then."

"Good man."

Danny went to get Ginny the next morning after having confirmed with Doctor Johnson's office that he was releasing her. Mom said she didn't need to go along, she would make sure everything was ready at the house.

"Mom, you are welcome to come along. Everything is ready here."

"That's ok. I might make a batch of no bake cookies for Ginny."

"Well, she does love those. If you're sure..."

"I'm sure. Go get them!"

When he left, she got on the phone and called Ted. "He has gone to get Ginny. Come on over."

While she waited for Ted, she went to her cottage and got the cake she had made last night and decorated with white and blue icing. She put it on the coffee table with plates and forks. She had ginger ale chilling in the refrigerator.

A short time later, Ted arrived. She opened the door so he could carry the cradle in. He sat in near the coffee table.

"Ted, it looks absolutely beautiful. I can't wait for them to see it."

Danny and Ginny pulled in the drive and Ted and Mom jumped to their feet and stood near the coffee table. Danny opened the door and helped Ginny in. She had the baby in her arms.

Ted and Mom whispered, "Surprise!"

Ginny took a few steps into the room and saw the cake, then she saw the cradle. "Oh, my word! What is this?"

Danny said, "I've seen this before. But I don't remember it looking this nice."

Mom burst out, "Ted refinished it. I've been waiting to show it to you!"

"Well Ted it's just beautiful!

Ginny agreed. "Mom was that Danny's cradle?"

"Yes, and mine. It was fairly scuffed before Ted took it to clean it up."

Ted said, "Enough of that, let me see my nephew!"

Ginny laughed and stepped over by Ted, "Wallace, meet Uncle Ted."

"How do, Wally old man!"

Ginny rolled her eyes. Danny said, "We knew he would be called Wally. We might as well get used to it."

Mom said, "Of course he's Wally, we can't call this tiny baby Wallace. He will grow into that."

"Yes, like how I grew into Daniel."

"We will all call you Daniel now if you like," Mom said.

"No, I suppose I'm fine with Danny."

Ted had also had a tiny mattress made to fit the cradle and Mom had covered it with a clean pillow case. They put Wally down in his cradle wrapped in a blue shawl. He was so beautiful. "Danny, grab the camera. I think we need a picture for the baby book. It's title will be 'Baby's First Home'."

# 27

## Mother's Story

Chet and Greta's two babies were happy and healthy and now Ginny and Danny had a healthy boy. JT's passing had left all of the assets in her control. Life had changed very rapidly.

She said all of *the* assets, not *his* assets. She wasn't sure he had ever improved their lot at all. He had the store when they first were married and it was paid off completely, but somehow, even though he bought merchandise and sold it at a mark up he never seemed to make much money. She had always suspected that his mother had paid the store off for him. She didn't know how he could have done it based on sales.

Then, that day that she had come home and found out he had traded the store and *all* of her money for this blasted farm. A run down house, fencing that was dragging the ground in more places than not and a few head of grade cattle. It was true that most of the acreage was good pasture, and the creek was never dry. But JT had never seen the place when he signed contracts. She still didn't know why he had done it. To spite her, probably. Without Chet's work it would never have shown a profit.

JT worked Chet like a hired hand but paid him no wages. He ridiculed him over buying the property adjoining, because the bulk of it was rocky ridge and timber. But true to his nature, JT couldn't see the big picture. Chet purchasing that piece had secured another quarter mile of that spring-fed creek.

The same day JT had taken her life in town from her, caused her to leave all of her friends and a job she loved, he had also cost her a daughter. Ginny had started her plan to go to California as soon as JT made his announcement. She couldn't blame her, what life would she have had here on this farm?

It was never supposed to be this way.

She was going to school to become a teacher when she had met Alfred Masters. He, like Chet, made women swoon without really ever being aware of the affect he had on them. From the day they met she had been lost. He asked her to marry, and she forgot that she had ever wanted to be anything other than his wife.

She had been so amused to watch Chet and Greta acting out the same play that she and Al had. But if she had anything to say about it their story would have a happy ending.

Al was a good man. The crash in '29 wasn't his fault, and he had been a good provider until then. She wished that he had kept up premiums on his life insurance, but she knew he had done the best he could.

It broke her heart to leave her children when she went to school, but she would never let them live in the conditions she lived in. Ginny wanted to badly to go back to 'town', but the 'town' Ginny remembered was pretty houses with pretty lawns and sidewalks and parks. That was not where she had lived. After she paid tuition for school, she had a handful of change left to live on. She had started with all of the decent boarding houses in town and been turned down, so she went next to the not-so-decent boarding houses. She offered to cook and clean to pay her way.

The place that finally took her up on her offer, gave her a room behind the kitchen, which had been a storage room. There was no window, and it was really just a closet. There was a mattress on an old iron frame and a table. She was given one set of stained sheets, deemed not good enough for the paying guests. After her first night, she realized the mattress was riddled with fleas. She couldn't burn it, or she would have nothing to sleep on. She dragged it out into the alley the next day hoping the sunlight would help. She beat the mattress until her arms ached. That night she had fewer flea bites.

For that luxury, all she had to do was wash all of the linens for the guests and do the dishes. She carried trash to the bins in the alley and scrubbed the kitchen floor at night when she wouldn't be in the way. When classes started and she wasn't available in the middle of the day, they saved all of the lunch dishes for her to do when she got home. Sometimes she worked until midnight, before she finally got to her school books. She sat on the edge of her bed with the table pulled close as a desk. She had a small lamp that gave her just enough light to read.

No, she wouldn't have taken her sweet babies there, even though it meant leaving them on the farm. When her parents weren't satisfied with the work she did over the summer and had asked her to pay for the children's upkeep, she was outraged. Poor little Ginny was working hard, too. She was trying to get an education to provide for her children, but her parents wanted her to either stay there and work for them or pay them.

She packed them up and went to Al's parents. She should have gone there first. She still had to leave them to go back to school but at least they weren't used as free labor.

Poor little Ginny still begged to go with her, but she would never have left Chet behind. She loved her little brother so much.

Another year of school and flea bitten nights and she got to see her babies again.

Then she finally graduated. Ginny was so sure that was when they would finally go with her and be a family again. It broke her heart to see the look on Ginny's face. She felt so betrayed, and nothing would convince her otherwise. She just couldn't understand that as a beginning teacher Mother couldn't afford an apartment for all of them, and she had no one to leave the children with during the day. She had hoped to find a position closer to the children so she could visit more through the year, but the higher-paying jobs were all too far away. She needed the money.

She did get to move into a slightly better boarding house and didn't have to wash dishes to earn her keep. Near the end of the school year, she had actually saved a little money.

Enter JT Smith.

JT Smith was older, he owned his own store and she met him in church. He courted her for months, but her only love had been Al Masters, so she didn't make it easy for him. She went to his store, and he asked her if she would like to see his living quarters. She didn't feel it was appropriate, but he assured her he would stay in the store, and she could look at the apartment all on her own. She had been curious, so she went up the stairs.

She was surprised. The apartment was large, it ran the entire length of the building, including the storage rooms in the back, so it was larger than the store. It had three bedrooms and a very modern kitchen and bathroom. It was well furnished, even though it could have used a woman's touch.

Near the end of the school term, she was planning for her summer on the farm, but looking for a small, furnished apartment that would be available when she came back for the next school year. This was the last summer that she planned to spend on the farm. She would wait to move the children to town until the school term started, so she could save that much rent money, but this was the year that she could have her children with her. Chet was ready to start school, so she wouldn't need to hire help to care for him. The children would go to the school were she was teaching, so they would be together. Money would be tight, but she could do it. Not quite as nice a neighborhood as Ginny remembered, but respectable.

JT Smith.

She had let it slip that she was looking for an apartment to bring her children to live with her. He pounced like a cat on an unsuspecting mouse. He proposed marriage, and when she showed her surprise, (shock, horror, mild disgust) he assured her that he understood that he could never replace the late Mr. Masters, to her or the children, but that he could provide them with a home, stability, and a respectable family life.

She fell for it. The only way she could forgive herself is that she was so very tired. She had worked for three years to set aside enough money to finally have her children with her, but it was a risk at that. She had barely enough to make ends meet and didn't see a possibility of saving more, once she had the children with her.

She said yes.

JT saw no reason to wait. They were married the day after the school year ended in a small but very proper church wedding, with a few close acquaintances as witness.

She asked when they could go gather the children.

"Oh, I won't be going with you. I have a store to run. I'm sure you had an idea of how to bring them here, just do as you had planned."

"Since I don't drive, I was hoping we could use your truck for the move."

"*Mrs. Smith,* I think you need to learn that business comes first. I need to run the store, and that truck is for store business, not for running to the country."

"Yes, JT." Lord, how many times had she said 'yes JT' over the years? Too many.

She was humiliated to tell her children and Al's parents that she had remarried without a husband by her side. She made excuses for him. She could see the disapproval in her mother-in-law's face, particularly when she said she would continue teaching. She felt judged as a mother and that she wasn't being judged fairly. She wanted to be a wife and mother first, but she had been forced to make a career for herself. JT said if she wanted her children to have nice things, she would have to keep earning. She couldn't expect his store to make enough for them all.

She was already feeling afraid that she had made a mistake, but she was sure of it when she introduced the children to JT. He had told her he would be a father to her children, but he made it clear then that he wanted no part of it. To be honest, Ginny didn't want to call him Papa, and if she didn't Chet wouldn't, but she thought JT would be *honored* to be their Papa. He dismissed them without even talking to them.

For the next few years, she bit her tongue and played the good wife, JT wanted children of his own, so she endured his fumbling attempts at getting one. Fortunately, he didn't have much more interest in her than she had in him, so those attempts were not all that frequent. Apparently, he had no notion that increased attempts would increase the odds of conception, and she didn't enlighten him. He just blamed her for being 'barren' and that she had 'mislead him' because she had children, and he thought she would have more.

He started a bank account for them to save money for the future. She dreamed of a house in one of the nice neighborhoods, that they could own, not rent, and she enjoyed seeing the bank balance grow. JT didn't contribute all that much to the account. He said she just didn't understand business, he had to have 'ready money' to pay his vendors, and he paid for their personal groceries from the store, too. She ignored his business and focused on her own job and her children.

She tried to make up to them for the lost years, but they didn't forgive easily, and JT wouldn't allow her to 'coddle' them. She tried to do as many nice things for them as she could. At least JT didn't mind that she bought them good clothes. He wanted to appear as the perfect family, and he wouldn't have them in worn clothes or hand-me-downs.

Then after all of the years of playing along, working toward a better life, on the very night they were celebrating Ginny's graduation from high school, he informed them that he had bought a farm in Arkansas. She had planned to use some money from the savings account to help

Ginny start a good life. What ever she wanted to do, she would help her get her education and get a start on life.

She had hoped that as an adult she and Ginny would become close again. She wanted her to understand that she had done the best she could and that she had always had her best interest at heart. And then she found out that JT had taken all of her money. She couldn't do anything for Ginny now, Chet either. It was gone.

She saw then that Ginny was planning something. Maybe she would refuse to go to Arkansas and would stay in town to go to school. She had friends she might stay with. It wasn't that far to the farm in Arkansas, they would see each other. She would still find ways to help her daughter.

When Ginny announced at her birthday dinner that she was going to California (why couldn't they get through a dinner without an announcement?) her mother was disappointed, but she could see that it was a good solution. Thank God, that daughter of hers had at least inherited her ability to handle her money. She had managed to save a great deal. She may have gotten her father's good looks, but she had her mother's business sense.

So, Ginny had made her own way, and she had done well. A career of her own and a man that loved her and now a baby. She was so envious that she could spit that Mrs. Armbruster got to move in and play full-time grandmother, but she also knew that she couldn't just pick up and leave.

Besides, she had Chet and Greta's babies right here. Little Alton was the next great love of her life. Her little Al. He was Alton not Alfred, but he was her little Al. Al Masters lived on in his grandson. She had been truly surprised at how JT doted on the boy. He called him Jim-Boy which made her cringe almost as much as it did Greta. She didn't know why Chet had named the boy after JT. She supposed his need for a father had been great. Poor boy. JT never saw him as anything but free labor. But JT's fondness for Alton was obvious and that he had bought bonds for his future was altogether miraculous.

The years they had spent here on the farm, letting JT run things had been tedious. He watched Chet's success year after year and still belittled him. Chet had done well with less property to work with, while JT had been sitting on a gold mine and couldn't manage it properly.

All those years, she had gone to work, put some of her money in the joint account at the bank (but never all of it, that was a mistake she wouldn't make twice) and had been the dutiful wife, being seen with him at church functions and town events. Mr. and Mrs. JT Smith were pillars of the community. She had even finally gotten pregnant, which had made JT happy with her for a while until the child was stillborn. Losing that baby had broken her heart one more time. JT blamed her, that she couldn't do anything right, but she had two perfect children, so maybe it was him. If there was anything that lessened her pain it was that JT wouldn't get his child either. But it wasn't much help. No mother should lose a child.

JT brought it up every time he wanted to hurt her. Her lukewarm feelings for JT had hardened over the years into something more akin to hatred.

When she sat with JT in the hospital after his stroke, her plan took form. She talked to Doctor Jeffries about the chance that JT would make a full recovery. He said that in all likelihood JT would recover some of what he had lost but that there was not much chance he would fully recover. He thought it likely that he could live for years in much the same state he was in at that time. Mrs. Smith told the doctor that if she was going to provide the care her husband needed, she would need to have the right to make decisions for him. He agreed whole-heartedly and told her he knew how to get a judge to grant her what she needed.

As soon as she had the power of attorney in her hands, she contacted Mr. Selfridge and leased him the pasture he had been after for years. She didn't lease him all of it. She had plans for that property for herself and Chet.

She did spend money on JT's care. As a good and dutiful wife, it was expected, and she wouldn't give anyone the opportunity to say she was mismanaging *his* assets. Doctor Jeffries had done her a great favor when he recommended Mrs. Fleming. She had been such a blessing and now was the greatest friend she had ever had. She had taken care of JT with professional efficiency, but she had also seen how things were in the home. She, like so may women, had a husband that was not a great provider, but wouldn't be disgraced by allowing his wife to work. After his death from a lingering illness, she was able to find jobs caring for others.

She thought she wasn't needed after JT's death. That couldn't have been more wrong. Mrs. Smith would want Mrs. Fleming to stay with her for the rest of their lives. They were two old widows that understood each other.

Telling JT that she has seized the money, and the control was the best day of her life since meeting him. She told Chet that he would be running the property on the east side, right in front of JT so she could see his eyes pop. She thought he might have another stroke right there. But she didn't outline her whole plan in front of him. Let him think she just gave it to Chet. He didn't need to know she was investing in the improvements.

Chet had proven to be up to the task. He made excellent choices on livestock, as she knew he would, but he also took time to care for his family. Her regret was that neither of them had seen how hard Greta was working. To think they could have lost baby Cara. Greta was so young and so tiny, but she worked as hard as the men. It had made them think she was stronger than she was. She mustn't ever work that hard again.

After JT died and they found out about the bonds he had purchased for Alton, she made arrangements for the younger children and made a will to allow for similar funds for any future children.

But she hoped to live to see her grandchildren grow. She had not turned the property over to Chet entirely. It would be his someday, but this property represented all of her years of work, all of her savings. She had done it all for her children. Now, those children were grown, and doing well on their own, but she would make sure that they and her grandchildren would never have to sleep on flea riddled mattresses or leave their babies as virtual orphans.

With her head for business and Chet's understanding of livestock and land management, they would grow this place into what it could be, far beyond anything JT Smith could have dreamed of. And all as JT's loving widow. That was a laugh. She kept up the charade. She spoke of JT with dignity and soaked up the admiration about how well she had taken over running his farm, with Chet's help obviously. She was just a poor old widow.

She had been taking whatever profits she could get her hands on and investing them into certificates of deposit at the bank. They had higher yield than a savings account and as one reached maturity she rolled it into another. She continued to teach so that her retirement fund would be as full as allowed.

She still paid Mrs. Fleming a wage, but it was more of an allowance for her now. She knew that she would live her life her as part of the family. That's why she didn't mind at all taking care of Greta when it was needed. Those babies were her family too, and Chet and Greta treated her far better than her own daughter did. That girl had too much of her father in her, mores the pity.

It had been a long rough road, and she had lost her children's respect along the way, but maybe she could go some way toward regaining it.

# 28

# Chet and Ginny

They couldn't believe it was real. They had been to the funeral and just left the attorneys office after reading the will. But it still wasn't real.

In all the years since JT had died their mother had continued to surprise them. When she retired from teaching, she had often left Mrs. Fleming in charge of her household and come to California in the winter months to stay with Ginny and her family.

Danny and Ginny had improved on *Rancho de Armbruster* over the years, adding on two bedrooms and a bathroom to the main house and building a proper barn for the horses and burro that Danny had acquired. Ginny's Christmas trees lined the drive, one for every year they had lived there. Mom still lived in the cottage though they tried to get her to move in to the main house so they could keep a better eye on her. She wasn't as young as she used to be.

But Ginny's mother would board a Greyhound and make that long journey, to stay for two to three months every winter. In later years, she gave up on Greyhound and flew when making the trip. Chet nor Ginny could believe their mother would get on an airplane, but after her first trip, she told everyone all about it, saying "You'll love it! It's wonderful."

Chet had continued to build on to the cabin until it was a rambling log home, surrounded by porches. He and Greta were both happy they had stayed in the valley. They built a little gazebo up on the ridge to enjoy the view. The view was beautiful, but the finest part was looking down at their cabin and the barns and corrals and all they had built together.

Their families had continued to grow, Ginny and Danny had two more children, all two years apart. Two little girls, Myra and Cathy. Chet and Greta had another daughter, too, little Karen born almost seven years after Cara.

Their mother doted on the children. She read to them, let them paint pictures, made cookies with them and gave them clothes to play dress up. All of the children loved Grandmother and knew she loved them.

For Chet and Ginny, who had never felt wanted as children, this was the biggest surprise of all.

Mother had kept her illness secret for as long as she could. She had seen several doctors, and they all agreed the outcome would be the same. She had a very advanced cancer and even with treatment she was unlikely to survive. She refused treatment and kept her pain to herself for as long as she could. By the time she admitted that she was ill, there was very little time left. So, the whole family was in shock.

Today Chet and Greta, Danny and Ginny and Mrs. Fleming had gone to the reading of Mother's will. At Mothers request, the will was to be read only if they could all be together. She had made a provision for Mrs. Fleming to continue living in the house for the rest of her life. There was a fund set up to continue paying her salary. The rest of the will was straight forward. Except for the amount set aside to buy bonds for the grandchildren everything was split between Chet and Ginny. That wasn't surprising. The surprise was in how much there was to split. Chet ran the cattle business and knew they were doing well, but this amount was far beyond that. Chet got the two-hundred-twenty acres that he had been working for years and her part in the ownership of the cattle. She left Ginny the eighty-acres, which was still leased. She could keep it as an income property or sell it. The value of the properties was factored in to how the cash wash divided. There was so much cash. When she took her teacher's retirement she lived simply and managed to put some of it in savings every month. She never took any of the profits of the cattle business rolling it into savings and a few very safe investments. With the property and the cash Ginny and Chet had just become very wealthy.

They went back to Mother's house and sat around the table. Ginny and Chet were still in shock. They had learned over the years that their mother had a good head for business, but this was beyond what they expected. Why had she never remodelled her house? She still didn't have hot water or a bathroom. She had a wringer washer that filled with a hose and hung clothes on the line. The only money she ever spent was on traveling to see Ginny. Why didn't she do anything for herself?

Mrs. Fleming shook her head. "You never knew her at all. She did nothing for herself, ever. Only for you."


Ginny and Chet walked up the hill behind Chet's cabin. They sat in the gazebo and looked out at the valley. *Their valley*. They sat in silence for a good long while. Chet finally broke the silence, "Ginny did Mother love us?"

"I don't know Chet. I think maybe she did."

# Some notes on "Roots"

*R*oots in the Dust is the first book I ever published. I wrote it in a very short time, once I started writing, but the story had been rolling around in my head for years. A lot of the story comes from things I was told as a child, and I filled in blanks here and there.

I remember my mother telling me that she had first met my father on the sidewalk in Prairie Grove, Arkansas and looked into the bluest eyes she had ever seen and was hooked. A very romantic story that I always loved. I never thought to ask why she or my father happened to be in town that day or when they saw each other next. You just don't think to ask when you are a kid.

The story about my grandmother coming home from teaching school one day to find that her husband had traded the store for a farm in Arkansas....is true. I can't even imagine. I painted JT in a pretty bad light in this book, I don't think he was all bad really. I didn't find out until I was grown that he had been "rough" on my father, (that could mean a lot of things) but I remember him as a kindly old grandpa that died when I was rather young.

Grandmother did have to leave her children with grandparents when she went to college for her teaching degree. She told me often that after tuition was paid, she had 3 cents left to her name. Back in the 'good old days' people didn't explain things to children. I know that my father and aunt felt abandoned and never felt loved or wanted. I think my grandmother did love them, but she was of the Victorian era and didn't show her feelings. (More on that in my next book, *Secrets in the Cane*)

When I started this book, with Chet and Greta meeting in Grove, they were my main focus, but as the characters grew, I saw that the story of the siblings wanted to be told. The thread of truth that runs through this is that my father and his sister were best friends for their entire lives. I never realized that until near the end of my father's life, when I saw him with my aunt. They shared experiences that no one else could understand. They went in very different paths, but, truly, their bond was never broken.

I guess the last thing I want to say is to my family: If I got it wrong, I apologize. I used true anecdotes where I could and filled in with fiction. I wish I had asked more questions when I had people around to ask.

CAM

**The real 'Chet and Greta".**

# About the Author

Carol Ann Martin is a writer deeply rooted in the Ozarks. Living in a secluded cabin, on the property where she was raised, she draws inspiration from the area's rich history and rural life. Her novels transport readers back to the 20th century, bringing the past to life, inviting readers to experience the beauty and hardships of a bygone era. When not writing, she can be found poking around the local flea markets, or just hanging around the cabin with Mehmet, her Anatolian Shepherd.

In her first two books, "Roots in the Dust" and "Secrets in the Cane", Carol has based characters on members of her own family and has retold stories of their struggles living through hard times in the 20th century. The books are fiction, not at all intended to be biographical, but many of the tales come from the author's tendency, as a child, to eavesdrop on her elders a bit.